NUMBERS DON'T ADD UP

Book 1: The Revelation

Shweta

INDIA • SINGAPORE • MALAYSIA

ISBN 979-8-89186-592-1

Dedication

For Ma and Papa

CONTENTS

PREFACE

The seeds of this book were sown almost 5 years ago while discussing a story idea with my friend Sweta, who is a screenwriter. I wrote some 20 pages on her idea, a very basic storyline, gave it to her and promptly forgot about it. Or rather, tried to forget about it. But the story kept popping in my head repeatedly at the most inconvenient moments. Like when I was reading a book or watching a movie or writing a client copy or simply talking to someone. A scene would play out in my mind, which would be a perfect fit in the novel. It seemed the story wanted to be written and so, in Jan 2020, I picked it up and wrote a full draft. But I was not satisfied with what I had written, so the draft sat on my hard disk for months on end.

Time went by and the pandemic struck. The first wave and then the deadly second wave. I lost all my clients and had to make a fresh start in Aug/Sep 2021. All thoughts of writing and publishing fiction were driven out of my mind as I focused on building my writing business. To satisfy the book publishing bug, in Oct 2021 I published my second non-fiction book – 24 Hours are Enough. By this time the idea of picking up Numbers Don't Add Up again was scary. Because I felt I must have forgotten many of the nuances I had weaved in there. But clearly, I had not.

When I finally started with the second draft in March 2023, after my daughters kept asking me when I will complete the book, the story flowed. And it is here in your hands. There is so much more I wanted to write but did not, because that interfered with the main storyline. Maybe I will write a Book 2 about all the things that I left unsaid. Maybe I will not. But till then, enjoy this book.

Shweta

CHAPTER 1

30-01-2018

CM Residence, 9:30 AM

70 years is a long time. A foetus in the mother's womb becomes an old man, a newly constructed building is on its way to be identified as a heritage, critically acclaimed art gets forgotten and a country changes its course. India has also changed in myriad ways between 1948 and 2018 but one thing that has stood the test of time is the love for Bapu, father of the nation.

CM Shantanu was no different, except he had no patience. He hated to wait. He sat on the sofa in his living room in a highly agitated state; tapping his left foot against the sparkling white floor, drumming the armrest with his fingers in a rhythmic 1-2-1-2-1. Maitreyi kept stealing glances at her husband, getting more nervous every second. She could feel the tension building inside him, and knew he would explode any moment out of frustration. It was so uncharacteristic of his secretary Naveen to be late. And that too on such an important day. Finally, he arrived in a huff, sweating all over despite the cool weather, but before he could offer any explanation Shantanu got up and took long strides to the door. Impeccable in white starched kurta pyjama and black waistcoat, he looked as handsome as ever. Watching him disappear round the door, Maitreyi was jolted out of her reverie and ran after him with his briefcase. Today was no day to entrust these trivial things to the house helps. She gave it to Naveen and a glance passed between the two, leaving Naveen in no doubt that his boss was in the foulest of moods. He almost ran all the way to the car so that he could be there to open the door for him. Not that it was required of him, but still Naveen thought it would be a good way to extend the olive branch. However, Shantanu did not even seem to notice. As soon as they were seated, the cavalcade started out of the CM residence.

It was the 70th anniversary of *Shahid Diwas.* All preparations had been made at the Assembly. 98% turnout was expected. You could always count upon the oldest 2% to fall sick genuinely or be absent out of sheer boredom, what with more than half the assembly above 65 years of age.

10:35 AM

When the cavalcade reached assembly gates there was already the usual crop of journalists waiting. Or was it a bit more? Have they got wind that something special was underway? Shantanu shrugged and let it pass. He was concentrating only on the morning's proceedings. He was never a fan of the media and not much had changed since assuming office. A lot of them thrust the mic in front of him asking if he had anything to say but as usual, he had nothing to say. The journalists also did not pester him much; they had got used to his silence and near hatred of the media in the past three and a half years. Also, they had already got their sound bytes from the legislators preceding him.

Shantanu went straight to the Assembly Hall. He had planned to go over the morning's proceedings with his secretary once again but as he was already late, his mind was all messed up. When you are not used to being late, that is what happens, and that too on such critical occasions when being on time is so important. He decided it would be best to get on with the event. Timing was essential for impact and he did not want to jeopardize that. That is what he had always believed in - let your actions speak for you louder than any word you could ever utter. He wanted today's event to become a talking point. At least for a couple of days. That would give him a breather to handle the peasant problems that had erupted in his own constituency without any pressure or media glare.

The Assembly Hall was sparkling clean. Two huge white screens adorned the walls to both right and left of the speaker's chair. The speaker herself was sitting on the treasury bench; for once she was happy to abandon her chair!! Shantanu could not help but smile despite the stress. Exactly at 10:45 am the AV presentation on Bapu began. For a change there was pin drop silence in the Assembly, with everyone concentrating on the presentation. 15 minutes later the AV ended with Bapu's resonating Hey Ram. At the cue, everyone rose from their seats to observe one minute of silence.

It was a sight to behold. Mass of sparkling white kurta pyjamas, dotted only with a couple of coloured dresses, that too in loyal handloom khadi material and dull tones. Some members held onto their desks to steady themselves, so unused they were of standing still even for a minute. Some clutched dear mobiles as if to console themselves that there was life as usual after this 1-minute silence was over. They had no idea life was not to be as usual on the other side of this 1-minute silence.

Outside the Assembly, most of the journalists had sauntered to their favourite chai stall lining both sides of the gate. They had not been briefed about the program inside the Assembly Hall. So, despite internal information they had no idea how much time the proceedings would take. As it was *Shahid Diwas,* they expected the legislators to declare a holiday for themselves after paying due respect to Bapu. As there was no urgent discussion or bill pending before the house, the rest could be ignored. Since there were no elections on the horizon, it was not the time for legislators to show their enthusiasm. That is how the Indian parliamentary system works; dragging its feet lazily from one election to the next.

Precisely at the half-minute mark of a hushed silence, the Assembly Hall was filled with a deafening explosion, making the Assembly Hall's grand chandeliers shiver violently. The deafening cacophony erupted from within, as if some beast had broken loose from its fetters, transforming the stately chamber into a pandemonium.

With the raw instinct for survival usurping their political prudence, the legislators turned into scrambling civilians. A mad dash to the robust mahogany doors ensued, their years of dignified discourse forgotten in the primal need for escape. Some dived under the desks, their bodies shaking visibly, eyes wide with terror. Panic-filled cries for help echoed off the ceiling, blending with the eerie wail of alarms.

Billowing clouds of dense, acrid smoke invaded the hall, smearing its pristine walls black. The choking fog swiftly used up the oxygen, turning each breath into a battle. The dissonant orchestra of coughs and wheezes punctuated the still air, as if the hall itself were gasping for relief.

Lying strewn across the mosaic floor were the fallen bodies from the first row, a grim reminder of the day's horror. Whether they had succumbed to the traumatic shock or the brutal impact of the explosion was a mystery. Crimson splatters of blood smeared across the pristine white of their formal attire, a haunting testament to the carnage.

The gleaming marble floor now bore the sinister artwork of the incident: glass shards twinkling ominously, paper sheets fluttering like ghostly butterflies and the lifeblood of democracy - smeared and splattered. The chaos screamed of violence and spoke of a grotesque disruption of the order, a nightmare that had sprung to life within the austere assembly hall.

Outside, it was a worse pandemonium. In the mind of the journalists. As each one of them scrambled to catch the first bytes from the politicians bound to come out anytime, to capture the first images of traumatised people, which could then be beamed on their respective channels as breaking news. They were barred from going inside earlier. This sudden change in scenario maintained the status quo. They could not go inside even now. They begged, cajoled and threatened the security persons to let them go inside. Maybe it was for the best; no one could be sure about the true intentions of media persons. Whether they wanted to go out of kinship and help the needy, or just to ensure they were the first one to get breaking news could never be ascertained. So much for the fourth pillar of democracy!!

2:30 PM

CM's residence

No one had seen the CM coming out of the assembly. He sneaked out the back door; today was not at all a day he would have wanted to speak to the media.

His inner circle of cabinet ministers, secretary Naveen, police commissioner and a man dressed inconspicuously in a cream safari suit were sitting at the conference table in the office. None of them looked relaxed. The ministers were chatting among themselves in hushed tones, waving hands wildly. While the ministers talked of political ramifications, the men in uniform sat quietly, preparing themselves for the questioning that was inevitable following the CM's arrival. Probably they went through a possible line of interrogation in their own minds. Oh yes! that is what it was going to be; they were in no doubt about it. The CM had needed no formal training to assume the role of an interrogator and put the other person at the receiving end. From day 1 of office, he had been in control.

The two of them had thick files in front of them, which they were careful not to refer to with so many people around. Whether they were tempted to do so, no one could tell. They had an aura to maintain and with the secretary observing them so closely they could not show any signs of weakness. They sipped from the glass kept in front of them occasionally, making an elaborate routine out of it, just to kill time. They took care to cover the glasses again. The CM was a stickler; he would have observed something as minute as that and then scorned too.

Just then the door was thrust open and the CM walked in, escorted by the security. He asked them to wait outside; all four of them. Their leader tried to say something but Shantanu just raised his left hand without even looking back and that was the end of the matter.

CM was not his usual self. He looked pale, probably due to the blood loss, bandages on his forehead, a thick plaster on the throat, and left hand encased in a sling. He took long strides to his table, dragged the chair and sat down. No one spoke anything as he lowered his head, closed his eyes and interlaced all ten fingers while resting his hands on the table. Everyone bowed their heads and waited for the ritual to get over. It was hardly 10 to 12 seconds but the heavy pall of gloom seemed to have travelled from the assembly and settled in the room in those few seconds. Everyone stared at the folders in front of them.

Suddenly CM Shantanu opened his eyes and pulled the file in front of him even before his secretary could react, breaking everyone's reverie. His soft voice pierced the taut atmosphere of anticipation, "first police headquarters and now this."

Turning to the police commissioner he said, "What do you have to say to this Mr. Wankhede? You have not yet been able to solve the police headquarter bombing and here comes a new incident. And that too right in the Assembly Hall. I had to make an important announcement after the video presentation, but that has to now wait.

To the man sitting to his right in safari suit he said, "any intelligence available on this Mr Verma?"

Mr Verma: "Sir, a few weeks back we had got reports at the local level that someone was trying to hire people notorious for assembling IED devices. We were trying to ascertain the veracity of this before moving further. Right now, we cannot be sure of any connection but...."

The CM threw up his hands in disgust. Mr Verma stopped mid-sentence. But then seeing the inquiring look on the CM's face he continued, "Sir, we cannot do anything about such information if there are no names, no dates and no concrete details. Moreover, if someone is trying to assemble IEDs, we usually get simultaneous intelligence about map procurement, surveillance, vehicle movement, etc. However, as there was nothing like this, we had only this angle to follow and we were trying to..."

He was rudely interrupted by the Home Minister, "trying to do what Mr Verma? Why was this information not passed on to me or to the police? Have you forgotten that internally we are still on alert to solve the police headquarters attack?"

Mr Verma: "I could not do that without confirmation to even some degree from our end. Every day we get so many tip offs that eventually turn out to be false."

Mr Wankhede came to Mr Verma's rescue. "Correct," he said, "I second him here. We cannot pass on every bit of information to the home minister without being fairly sure it has at least some amount of truth in it."

Hearing all this banter, CM Shantanu suddenly lost his cool and snapped at the home minister: "Have you had a briefing from them? Just tell me the gist of it."

Home Minister: "Sir, as per reports, there was no prior intel that any attack was being planned. Also, due to lack of intelligence from the IB or the RAW, we can rule out involvement of terrorists."

CM shook his head and said, "Don't be hasty in dismissing anyone at this stage. Two explosions in 6 months. Do you think a local outfit is capable of managing this? Without the police or the intelligence getting a wind of it?"

He then asked the police commissioner who was in charge of the incident at the assembly.

Police commissioner: "SP Ajay, sir. It falls under his PS."

CM: "At least you have something positive going on, even if by default. Ask him to meet me with the preliminary report. I want daily reports for the next 7 days. And by that time, you should be able to tell me who was behind it. Now both of you can go back to your offices and resume your work. I do not need to tell you that this is a priority. We cannot tolerate such blatant threats to democracy."

Mr. Wankhede and Mr. Verma picked their files, mumbled their thank you's and hurried out. Being dismissed so summarily was insulting but over a long career they had got used to being treated rudely by politicians in power. The only solace was that they did not last long; at least not longer than the bureaucrats themselves.

Meanwhile, a heated and passionate discussion resumed in the CM's office.

Minister 1 - with byelections just eight months away, we must solve this quickly.

Minister 2 - yes, we cannot let the opposition use this opportunity to point out our inability to maintain law and order in the state. Police headquarters was different.

With an attack on their own territory, they are bound to be touchier.

The CM listened to all opinions attentively without interrupting anyone. But soon, the voices seemed to fade away and he was lost in memories and thoughts of his own. His secretary observed this and realized there was no use for this pretence of a meeting anymore. He whispered in his ears to break his reverie.

CM said to the assembled group – "let us stop this discussion here for the day. We will wait for some reports tomorrow. It will be intimated to you and if needed we will have a meeting again to discuss the development. Naveen will inform you about the details. Meanwhile, please no loose comments to the media. I should not need to remind you of this but unfortunately, I have to due to the past record."

The ministers walked out of the office whispering among themselves. The CM then addressed Naveen – "let us get to work now. Bring those files we had marked for today."

Naveen looked uncertain. Finally, he said, "without the announcement today, does that make sense?"

"We will find the right opportunity for that, do not worry. Let us complete the groundwork so that we can move in quickly without giving the detractors a chance."

"But you should take a rest at least for today. The doctor says you have lost lots of blood and…" CM interrupted Naveen with a wave of his hands, "the doctor does not run this state, Naveen. Already there is so much pressure."

And then seeing the look of concern on Naveen's face, he added softly, "I will take a break if I feel tired. Promise."

CHAPTER 2

30-01-2018 Around 10:30 AM

Commanding the room from his perch on the edge of a grand mahogany table, Ajay toyed absentmindedly with a sterling silver paperweight. His gaze, sharp as an eagle's, bored intensely into the man seated across him. Sweat began to glisten on the man's forehead, each droplet reflecting Ajay's silent interrogation. The grandfather clock on the wall conducted the silence, ticking seconds into minutes, its rhythmic beat only amplifying the tension that wound the room tighter and tighter.

Karuna, the stern and seasoned head constable, stood a little apart, her arms folded across her chest. As the standoff drew on, she found it increasingly difficult to believe that Ajay's audacious terms would be conceded. Her trained eyes studied the setting, the grim lines of her face etching deeper with each passing second.

Suddenly, the whole room exhaled as the man across Ajay released a long, pent-up breath, as if he had been holding the world inside his lungs. His fingers, pale and trembling, relinquished the grip they had on the briefcase that had been his constant companion. It landed with a soft thud on the table before he snapped it open with a decisive click. Out came three bundles of crisp pink notes, their collective worth radiating an almost palpable energy. He pushed them across the table towards Ajay.

With a curt nod, Ajay signalled Karuna. Her hands, steady and practiced, picked up the fat bundles and locked them away in the impregnable safe built into the wall behind the table. Ajay's voice sliced through the thick silence then, his command as firm as the granite of the walls, "Escort *buddhe baba* out. After that, we'll decide what to do with *Gandhi Baba*." The cryptic statement hung in the air as Ajay slid from his perch and sauntered towards the garage. It was time for his morning rounds.

Just as he disappeared from view, the shrill ring of the telephone shattered the lingering silence. Karuna was closest. She glanced at the empty space Ajay had occupied, then moved to pick up the receiver. As she listened, all colour drained from her face, her normally composed features succumbing to shock. The erratic, incomprehensible chatter from the other end reached Ajay, who had turned back at the sound of the ringing. He covered the distance in long strides, taking the phone from Karuna's trembling hands. His commanding presence filled the room once again, as he steeled himself to decipher the chaos unfolding on the other end of the line.

"Be calm and then tell me from where you are speaking?

ok, briefly describe what has happened?

ok we are on our way."

Ajay's voice, steady as the rhythm of the grandfather clock adorning one of the walls, resonated through the receiver. He carefully returned the phone to its cradle with a faint click, the cacophony from the other end silenced. With a contemplative look on his face, he pushed himself up from the chair, its leather groaning as his weight was released.

His words then cut through the room's heavy silence, directed towards everyone yet no one in particular. "There's been a blast at the Assembly. We must leave immediately." He announced, as if he was merely commenting on the weather.

To an outsider, it might have seemed as though Ajay had anticipated this news, such was his unruffled demeanour. But this was quintessential Ajay. His serenity a steadfast ship in the storm of crisis. The deeper the trouble, the more profound was his tranquillity, as though calamity was a stimulant for his calm. A paradox. But then, Ajay was a man of paradoxes.

He was acutely aware of the mounting pressure that was about to engulf the entire police department. The Assembly was a fortress of security and its breach represented an unthinkable failure. As the officer in charge, Ajay knew he would bear the brunt of the investigation and the storm of questions that would follow. The thoughts of impending pressure tightened his chest, but like a seasoned policeman that he was, he prepared to navigate through the turmoil. His character, shaped by adversity and tough experiences, now stood ready to face whatever was to come next. He had chosen this difficult posting just after 7 years because he wanted his mettle tested. More by his own standards than others.

As Ajay, flanked by Karuna and their squad of ten hardened policemen, reached the Assembly, an unprecedented scene of panic and fear unfolded before them. A good half-hour had passed since the blast but chaos thrived in the very place where law and order were supposed to reign.

Thankfully, amidst the chaos and pressure of frantic people moving all over the place, the security personnel had not lost their heads. They had been stopping people from entering the Assembly. They had held the line, allowing those within to escape, but denying entry to those who were desperate to get in.

Ajay, his eyes quickly assessing the situation, signalled a pair of his men to strengthen the human barricade at the entrance. He wanted to prevent both entry and exit until they had a firm handle on the situation. Like a well-rehearsed drill, the policemen fell into position, cordoning off the area and pushing back the swelling tide of onlookers and anxious family members.

With the imposing edifice of the Assembly looming before him, Ajay led his team towards the Assembly Hall. The burnt air, heavy with dust and despair, stuck in their throats as they ventured deeper into the ravaged Assembly. Ajay tasked Karuna with the responsibility of cordoning off the hall's entry, her firm nod echoing her understanding of the gravity of the situation. It was always a relief to have Karuna around, so well she understood the unspoken and the undercurrent.

Ajay moved cautiously, his boots tip-toeing against the marble floor, stained with the aftermath of destruction. His eyes were drawn towards the well at the centre, probably the epicentre of the explosion, an abyss of charred debris and splintered furniture. The front row of benches, once seats of power, lay twisted and blackened, a macabre sculpture of violence.

Silhouettes of crouching legislators, frozen in their hiding spots under the benches, dotted the landscape of the hall. A sight of their khaki uniform must have sparked relief in the terrified lawmakers, but shock pinned them to their hiding spots. Ajay's team methodically approached them, guiding them out from the sides and back of the benches, their voices a soothing balm amidst the terror.

Throughout, Ajay's voice echoed like a mantra, reminding everyone to avoid stepping into the blasted well. Every piece of shattered marble, every singed piece of fabric was a potential clue, a piece of a jigsaw puzzle that could lead them to the perpetrators.

Just as he was contemplating summoning the bomb squad, the piercing trill of his phone sliced through his thoughts. The display revealed the caller – the police commissioner himself. Ajay's jaws hardened as he prepared himself for the conversation that was to follow. He took a final glance at the disaster zone and then accepted the call, his voice steady, his resolve unwavering.

Wankhede: "Where are you, Ajay? What is the situation there?"

Ajay: "Sir, I have just reached. We have cordoned off the building as well as the Assembly Hall. All the people still inside are being evacuated. Those who needed first aid have been sent to the hospital. I have also secured the well of the Assembly because it seems that the bomb went off in that area. Sir I think we should call in the Bomb Squad to take evidence. We are not trained to do that. It being the Assembly, the case will be highlighted everywhere; we must take every step cautiously from the start. Meanwhile, I will gather whatever information I can from the people here."

Wankhede: "Ok, I will send the bomb squad. I was also thinking on the same lines but wanted a confirmation from the scene before doing anything. I do not need to emphasize the importance of this investigation to you Ajay. But still I will add, it is going to be politicised to the hilt. So please take utmost care not to ruffle feathers but be thorough while interrogating too. You might not get a chance to talk to these people again."

After disconnecting, leaving Karuna in charge of the evacuation and medical assistance, Ajay walked over to the adjacent room where the rest of the legislators, almost 180 of them, were seated. All of them sat there scared shitless. Looking at them no one would have guessed that they were one of the most powerful people of the state. Right now, they felt lost and did not know how to react. When Ajay walked into such an atmosphere, most heaved a sigh of relief but some felt irritated that they would have to talk to police in such a disoriented state of mind. None of them were strangers to police and policemen. But they had usually dealt with them from a position of strength. However, right now they felt vulnerable. We humans get so used to wielding power over others that we hate being soft and vulnerable. We fear others will take advantage of our situation, probably because that is the way we ourselves behaved in the past.

Ajay asked after their well-being generally and tried to calm them down. He then announced that they would be asking each of them some questions to help in the investigations. He wanted to record each of their versions so that he could piece together the complete truth from fragmented narrations. He could see resentment rising on some of their faces but before they could voice their reservations or objections, he requested them to cooperate so that the culprit could be nabbed without delay. Walking out of the room he called three of his best men and asked them to set up interrogation tables in three different rooms and interrogate all of them one by one. "All of them Sir? There are so many," said Rohan with a start. Ajay gave him a dirty look and said, "yes, each one. Why, do you have to be anywhere else right now?" Realising he might have been too hard on him, Ajay added, "do you realise the gravity of the situation Rohan? It is the assembly. The seat of power. And still someone or some people had the guts to do this in broad daylight. We must find the culprits immediately. And as these people were present at the scene, their information can be a good starting point. We must record their statements before the small details begin escaping their memory. Let us prepare a list of questions for them." With this he sat down at one of the tables, with pen and paper and started listing the questions. Once he was through, he asked them to make three copies quickly and go to their seats. Then he assigned two men to be stationed in the room and send the legislators one by one for questioning. By this time Karuna re-joined them because the evacuation of the hall was complete. He asked her to monitor the interrogation to ensure it went smoothly and none of them left the assembly antagonised. He himself walked casually down to the security guard standing at the gate of the assembly building.

Ajay decided to get the preliminary information by himself so that it could be verified against the legislators' version. The guard told him that a video presentation was going on inside the hall because he could hear the voices coming out from there. Ajay made a mental note to get hold of the presentation later and see what it was all about. The guard further added that when the presentation was over there was complete silence for a couple of minutes and then suddenly a huge explosion was heard. He rushed inside to see what had happened. Before rushing in he had asked his partner to remain at the gate and not allow anyone inside. He said that they were given regular training about what to do in case of a sudden incident. Ajay behaved as if he was very impressed by all this and wanted to know more. The guard went on to narrate the pandemonium that ensued, both inside the hall and outside the building, in the aftermath of the explosion.

Thanking the guard for a great job done, he moved towards the group of journalists standing in a huddle just outside the gates. He asked them for their version of the incident. This was the information that he could gather from the general questioning:

They had been waiting for the politicians to arrive since 10 o'clock in the morning. Given some time, and if needed, they could recreate the arrival sequence of many of the politicians. Most of them had moved away to the tea stalls just outside the boundary after the program had begun inside at around 10:50. They were chatting when they heard a huge explosion from the assembly building and rushed back. They could hear some cries for help from inside but they were not allowed to go in because they did not have the permission for the event. The guard had been instructed that no one was to enter the premises and he was very stubborn about it.

Ajay realised that there were just two journalists who were present within the premises when the explosion took place. He took them aside and questioned them individually. His assistant religiously took down every word as he had been doing since they had arrived at the scene.

Once Ajay was sure that they could not tell him anything more, he decided to go inside to check on the progress of interrogation.

Just as Ajay was about to go inside, a huge white van with reinforced protection screeched to a halt just inside the gates. The bomb disposal squad had arrived. They were an elite branch of police specialising in diffusing bombs as well as collecting forensic evidence after an explosion. They had arrived at the scene in record time. Usually, they were so short of manpower that hours would pass before they appeared. But this was a high priority case. Explosion in the Assembly could not be taken lightly. The Commissioner must have spoken to them about expediting things. Ajay wanted to know who was the team leader and so he waited. He would have to coordinate with them for this case, so it was better to know what to expect. He did not know many men from the Bomb Squad, so he was a bit apprehensive. In their field of duty, they could not choose their partners but everyone wanted to work with people with whom they would be comfortable.

But that was not to be so in this case of all cases.

When Ajay saw Satyarthi getting down from the van, he froze for a second. Their eyes met and he could feel the frost in those deep brown eyes. Eyes that always haunted him and reminded him of someone else.

CHAPTER 3

30-01-2018, 10:30 AM, Bomb unit, Police Headquarters

Satyarthi was in a meeting discussing their latest case. They were on the verge of concluding their investigation and he felt that an all-hands meeting would help them reach the conclusion faster by considering everyone's perspective and eliminating any scope for error.

The case room was a spacious area located at the far end of the Bomb Squad offices. With its sterile white walls, bright LED lighting and giant pin-up boards covering two sides of the room, it had an unmistakable investigative aura.

Bang in the middle of the back wall was a five-foot-wide map of the commercial complex that had been bombed just two days ago. The complex housed a popular cinema hall on the ground floor and a children's activity centre on the first floor. The two bomb blast sites were marked with glaring red pins, stark against the black and white map.

Surrounding the map were dozens of printed photographs taken by the forensic team. The images showed the ripped-apart ticket counter at the cinema hall entrance and the collapsed roof of the children's centre. Shocking glimpses of blood-spattered walls, severed limbs and anguished faces told the horrific story in graphic detail.

Below the photos were the names and mobile numbers of the investigating officers handling the blasts case, written in bold black letters. At the top was 'ACP Satyarthi Kumar.'

Satyarthi sat at the head of the long mahogany table, a grave expression on his rugged face. His team of eight talented officers sat along the sides, case files and notepads open in front of them. There was an urgency in the air – they felt so close to a breakthrough, yet it evaded them. Satyarthi was confident that the evidence was right there in front of their eyes, even if elusive.

"Let's start from the beginning once more," Satyarthi said, his voice crisp and authoritative. "Sohail, summarise the case details again for everyone."

Sohail nodded, clearing his throat. In his precise, methodical way, he briefly went over the facts gathered so far. The bombs had been assembled with deadly sophistication using RDX, suggesting the handiwork of trained terror groups. CCTV footage showed four men in black entering the complex thirty minutes before the blasts. No concrete leads yet on their identities.

They had been working in teams of 2, following different leads of the case. Satyarthi now signalled to the first team to share their findings.

But before anyone could start, the peon rushed into the case room, breathless. "Sir, urgent call for you from the Police Commissioner!" he announced.

Satyarthi looked at the telephone in the corner of the case room briefly. That the police commissioner had not asked to be transferred to this number meant that he had something confidential to tell him. With a grim face, he strode into his chamber and picked up the receiver.

As Satyarthi listened intently, his already stern features grew taut, thick eyebrows drawing into a deep frown. The occasional "Understood sir," and "Right away, sir," were the only interruptions to the Commissioner's intense briefing.

Taking long strides, he hurried back towards the case room, his mind racing, his team awaiting his return eagerly, their discussion interrupted at a critical point. But now there would be none.

There was no time to be lost in calling them to his room and then briefing them. An explosion had occurred inside the Assembly, and a more powerful bomb seems to have exploded right in the police commissioner's lap, going by the urgency and hysteria in his voice. He wanted everything to be done now. Better still, yesterday.

"There's been a blast at the Assembly Hall," Satyarthi announced abruptly. "Gear up to move out immediately." Straight to the point as always.

He further instructed his second in command, Sohail, to round up the best people and start in 10 minutes. "I want 10 people at least," he emphasised.

His team sprang into action, experienced hands swiftly gathering equipment and securing firearms with smooth efficiency. Donning bulletproof vests and checking ammunition clips with trained speed, they were ready within minutes. The ten officers piled into the police van, mentally preparing themselves for the chaos and gore that awaited at the Assembly site.

Meanwhile, after giving instructions Satyarthi went back to his own room and flipped open the laptop lying on his table. He immediately logged into the database and opened the floor plan of the Assembly and its premises. He shot a printout and began studying it. Just then a constable came to inform that everyone was ready to move. He rolled up the map print out, put on his cap and was ready to go.

On sitting inside the van, he cross-checked if everyone had taken their safety gears. They always had to be ready for the probability that the site could hold some unexploded bombs. It was regulation to wear their safety outfit until that probability had been ruled out. Today they could not take chances. According to what he had gathered from Mr Wankhede, there had not been much casualties in numbers. And in his experience, this was surprising. If someone took so much pain to penetrate the Assembly, which could not have been easy, why stop at such minor explosion. He very much expected some unexploded arsenal as well. Hence the preparation.

At the venue, Satyarthi jumped down from the van, his sharp eyes already analysing the situation. Years of Bomb Squad experience had honed his ability to swiftly grasp emergency scenarios. The signs of panic were evident in the frightened faces and raised voices. Thankfully there were not too many people around. Because casualties happened more due to uncontrolled mobs than collapsing structures.

As he began firing quick directions, organizing his men on the ground, Satyarthi's gaze collided with Ajay's. For an instant, his inscrutable mask seemed to slip, as memories came flooding back and images flashed before his eyes. Images he had not been able to erase after so many years, however much he tried. But just as quickly, Satyarthi was back in control, his focus steely and unbroken. But the brief unguarded moment had not gone unobserved.

Sonia, a journalist from popular news channel *Khabarnama*, immediately sensed history between the two officers. She made a mental note to probe that angle if she got the chance. For now, she tried to push past Satyarthi, shoving her mic insistently forward.

Sonia had been trying to get inside the Assembly for the past one hour. But there had been no success so far. Although Ajay looked effusive and reachable, she had not been able to break through him. And he was so shrewd that no one could work around his arrangements. She knew about a small rickety gate at the back of the Assembly building but by the time the idea had struck her the barricading was already in place. Sonia was no newbie but she was not yet a veteran, having worked the crime beat only for the past 2 years. For a year before that she was covering city's social scene. However, as she always ended digging up the celebrity's secrets, her editor thought it prudent to put her on crime beat. Secret about celebrities' juicy stuff was welcome many times but not always broadcast worthy. One could not show all types of stuff on prime-time television. Despite the plummeting morals of the television news industry, there were still some things off limit. Especially adult stuff. You could not parade that in front of a family consisting of young impressionable minds and still expect to hold onto the audience. In crime stories, the focus always was on finding new angles and new leads, which Sonia was very good at.

Thankfully she was nearby when the explosion occurred and the newsroom was alerted. She received a call from her editor and reached the location in 7 minutes flat. She had not been able to gain any leeway till now but she was relentless in her pursuit.

She had noticed the exchange of glances between Satyarthi and Ajay. Clearly, the two had a shared past that still haunted them, Sonia deduced. She could recognize the signs, having done this for three years now. Her news instincts buzzed with anticipation. There was a complex history here waiting to be uncovered. She would have to dig deeper to unravel this mystery between the two cops, especially if she wanted exclusive scoops that would distinguish her reporting.

Human angle was always important in her stories because that is what made them so relatable for the common people. She decided to ask Satyarthi a few questions even though he had arrived on the scene just now. He must be having some information relayed to him, which she did not have. More than an hour had passed but there had been no official statement of any kind. Just as she was about to approach him, the back doors of the tactical van swung open, and a team of men clad in specialised gear descended, freezing her in her tracks. They were outfitted in bomb suits layered with Kevlar and flame-resistant material, helmets featuring reinforced visors, and utility belts teeming with an array of essential tools from wire cutters to rangefinders. Their bulky appearance belied a fine-tuned agility; their gloves were designed for both protection and the dexterity needed for the delicate task of bomb defusal. With a quick glance and a nod among them, their visors went down, sealing their silent pact of readiness and shared risk, making it clear that every element of their gear was optimized for extreme situations. Since coming here, Sonia realised for the first time that she really was on a bombing site and technically in danger until the whole area was swept and declared safe.

"Any comments for the media on the situation, sir? How many injured so far?" she asked rapidly. But Satyarthi brushed past her brusquely, moving with purpose towards where Ajay stood grim-faced at the building entrance. They shook hands perfunctorily but their tense body language indicated a strained relationship devoid of any real warmth.

Together they moved inside. Satyarthi pushed open the barricaded door and entered, Ajay following him cautiously, for he did not want to interfere with the forensic evidence inadvertently. Inside the hall, Satyarthi surveyed the devastation with an expert eye. The bomb had detonated right in the middle of the legislative well, tearing through the front benches. The weakened marble floor was littered with shrapnel, broken furniture, and shards of glass. Acrid smoke still lingered in the air.

The bomb seems to have been optimised for maximum effect not casualty. Anything that was a few benches forward would have left those seated at the back untouched. And anything two benches back would have spared the front benchers. Whoever had done this wanted maximum damage for the ruling party, this much was evident. That the CM was safe was a miracle. The bomb disposal team followed close on the heels of Satyarthi and Ajay. They divided into five teams of two each. Two of the teams set about sweeping the hall to ensure that there were no unexploded bombs around. The other three teams looked around the debris, collecting everything that remotely looked like pieces of bomb.

As Satyarthi watched his team meticulously comb through the debris, he noticed satisfactorily that one of his officers, Raghav, was meticulously studying the miniscule crater caused by the explosion. He was the newest member of the team but also the quickest learner. And may be that was the reason he had earned his place in the team for such an important case. With a laser rangefinder, Raghav measured the diameter and depth, jotting down the figures in a dedicated logbook. These measurements would later help explosives experts estimate the charge size and the type of container used, essential clues in identifying the bomb-maker's modus operandi.

"Cordon off this area," Satyarthi said to Ajay, his tone clipped and formal. "No one should be allowed near until our work is complete."

Ajay nodded, avoiding his gaze as he relayed orders to his constables. Their interactions remained strictly professional, almost painfully so. But despite everything, Ajay was fascinated by what was going on in front of his eyes. This was not the first time he was so closely seeing the Bomb Squad in action. But still he was riveted, to say the least.

He watched keenly as a woman used a portable gas chromatograph to sample the air for residue chemicals. Ajay knew that the device was capable of detecting minute amounts of substances used in bomb-making, such as ammonium nitrate or RDX. Although the blast would have burned away most of the evidence, a skilled operative could still pick up trace amounts that could serve as vital leads.

Behind him a pair of officers were engaged in sifting through debris using specialized sieves. They were looking for bomb components that might have survived the explosion—anything from timer pieces, battery parts, to fragments of the detonation mechanism. Every tiny piece was a puzzle element that could help them piece together the type of device used, and possibly lead them back to the perpetrators. Their effort would bear fruit in less than 24 hours.

"Label and bag those fragments carefully," Satyarthi directed. And then mumbled to himself, "each one could be the smoking gun we need to break this case," as officers put recovered pieces into evidence bags, sealing them with tamper-proof tape and attaching pre-coded barcodes for easy cataloguing later.

Satyarthi seemed satisfied with his team's progress. He kept a continuous eye on Sohail, who was coordinating the scene's photographic documentation that would allow them to recreate a virtual model of the crime scene later, useful for both ongoing investigation and court testimony.

It took them majority part of the day to complete their work. By that time Ajay's team had also completed their interrogation of the surviving members. He went inside the room to thank the legislators and Assembly employees for their cooperation. He also reminded them that if required he would get in touch with them to verify some of the facts.

There was nothing left to do right now. So, Ajay rounded up his team and asked them to start getting into their vehicles. Just as he was about to go out of the building, Satyarthi came up to him, as if he wanted to speak something but was in two minds. Ajay could read the hesitance.

He himself asked him, "is your work over? Can I ask my boys to remove the barricades?"

Satyarthi had an unexpected request. He asked Ajay to keep the Assembly Hall locked and in his custody. He wanted that the room should not be handed over for cleaning until and unless Satyarthi gave the go ahead. Ajay was perplexed and said as much. They had collected all evidence. There did not seem much sense in what he was asking. But Satyarthi felt he might need to come back to the site after the preliminary investigation of the evidence collected by his team today. As it was such a high-profile case, he did not want to goof up knowingly. Ajay instructed one of his boys to put lock on the hall, seal it and hand over the keys to him. As he was officially in charge, he kept the keys with himself even though Satyarthi wanted it. He assured Satyarthi that he will get it whenever he wanted, whatever the time of day or night. Not looking satisfied with the arrangements but accepting it nonetheless, Satyarthi walked towards the vehicle where his team was already boarded.

All this while, Sonia hovered at the periphery, biding her time. She would unlock the secrets between these two officers even if she had to stake out their office doors, she vowed silently. After all, conflict and ties from the past almost always came back to haunt the present. That was the one absolute truth she had learned from years of covering crimes and celebrities before that. This story was far from over.

CHAPTER 4

30-01-2018, 6:20 PM, Police headquarters

Both Ajay and Satyarthi stood before the Police Commissioner Mr Wankhede. He was immersed deeply in reading the file in front of him. He had not asked either of them to sit, which was unusual. He always came across as a reasonably courteous man. But today he seemed worked up. The lines on his forehead were even deeper, the crows' feet more pronounced as he tried to concentrate. After some time, he lifted his head from the file and looked at both ponderingly. I am putting both of you on this case, he said abruptly. There was a quick intake of breath that did not reach him. And it is good that it did not, because nothing could dissuade him from his decision. The pressure was simply too much. He said, "Ajay, you will be reporting to the CM directly whenever he wants. But I want you to brief me beforehand about what you are going to tell him. And after each meeting you let me know if there was anything more. Although Satyarthi is senior to you, I am giving you this responsibility because you are better in handling people, especially those in power."

He turned to Satyarthi and continued, "that does not mean you will be absolved of all responsibilities of dealing with people. When it comes to media you will have to appear because they are a pack of wolves we cannot afford to let loose. When they see a senior bomb expert working on the case, they might be pacified for the time being.

And I have seen how expertly you handled them during the Police HQ bombing. The ministers and the whole government are already breathing down my neck, I do not want the media to add to my woes."

CM residence, 10:45 PM

Ajay sat in front of the Chief Minister across his table. His PA Naveen was present, as always. Seeing the chief minister all bandaged up, right hand in a sling, Ajay realised that he had to take his statement as well. After all he was present in the Assembly during explosion and he was a survivor. Being an intelligent and observant person, he could shed some light on what could have happened. Ajay decided to wait for his report to be over before questioning the CM.

"So, what are you people up to?" the CM asked, eyes piercing into Ajay's. "Have you got any leads? Any idea who could be behind the explosion?"

"Sir, we've taken statements from all surviving legislators," Ajay began, but was cut off.

CM, raising an eyebrow: "Except mine."

Ajay: "I was getting to that sir. But first the report. The bomb squad has collected preliminary forensic evidence from the site and they have sent it to their experts for analysis."

CM (impatience evidence in his manners): "I want answers Ajay, and that too quickly. If possible, within this week."

Ajay: "I promise we are doing our best, sir. The paperwork is holding us back a bit. There is so much of official paperwork and reporting involved that I have not yet got the opportunity to sit down with all the evidence and analyse them. We will let you know as soon as we get a breakthrough."

CM: "I understand Ajay what you are trying to say but it is necessary to keep others informed as well. I must answer to so many people even though I am the chief minister. In fact, sometimes I feel that being the Chief Minister I must be more accountable to the people. We managed the official statement today without much substance because it was the first day and no one was expecting anything concrete. However, as the days go by, people want results. They want to know who was behind this. The legislators want to know who was audacious enough to target their lives."

Ajay: "I understand Sir. I will report to you every day. However, there was a request. Is it possible to give you the report on the phone sir? Coming and going takes lots of time. If there is anything confidential, I will come."

CM: "OK Ajay. Take Naveen's number and call him. He is always there with me so you will be able to you talk to me."

Then he added, in a lighter note, "except between 12 at night to 8 in the morning when he is supposed to be at home."

Ajay: "Thank you sir. Now can you please tell me if you saw something today morning that you think could be related to the case?"

CM, concentrating hard: "I do not think so Ajay. I was already running late, all thanks to Naveen here. Panditji had already told me it was an inauspicious day so I had to make doubly sure that everything went smoothly. All my focus was on getting to the Assembly in time. I had organised the whole show, so I could not afford to be late. (pondering) I think that by the time I reached, almost everyone was in place. (Looking at Naveen) as far as I remember, only Mr Kelkar, the leader of opposition came in 5 minutes after me."

Ajay: "And after the explosion?"

CM: "Well, at that point of time all of us were standing, our eyes closed. I also did not see anything."

Shantanu got up from his chair and started pacing the office in slow laborious gait. The effect of painkillers seemed to be waning. He decided to ask Naveen for more once Ajay was gone.

To Ajay he said, "That is why I never do anything without consulting our auspicious charts. But this is something that could not have waited for an auspicious date. Martyr's day must be celebrated on Martyr's Day itself. If only I had followed my heart, maybe this tragedy could have been averted."

Hearing the CM expound on importance of astrology and numerology made Ajay impatient and moody. He literally locked his hands at his back to prevent himself from throwing them up. The logic of auspicious and inauspicious dates was completely beyond him. His colleagues and subordinates often called him an atheist due to his beliefs. And here was the state Chief Minister thinking that a tragedy could have been averted if only he had listened to the astrologers before organising an event!! The only word that came to his mind was 'ridiculous.' Unfortunately, he could not speak his mind. Exercising supreme control on his itching tongue, he managed to get Naveen's phone number and escape from there. It was almost midnight by the time he hit the main road off CM residence but his day had not yet ended. He wanted to call up Satyarthi and enquire if he had got any breakthroughs but Ajay knew this would only show him to be restless and nothing else. Not even 8 hours had passed since the team had collected evidence. It was too soon to expect even preliminary hypothesis, let alone any results.

Ajay was driving himself. He had seen no point in asking someone to drive him after such a long day and dismissed his designated driver before going to the CM's residence. He knew he should go home now, but the prospect of going to an empty house felt unbearable. Meeting Satyarthi had made him even more aware of this stark reality. He kept driving aimlessly. Steering on instinct more than intention. He meandered through the labyrinthine streets until, almost as if drawn by some magnetic force, he found himself near the Assembly Building.

Ajay stepped out of his car, parked at a discreet distance from the Assembly Building. Caution tape fluttered in the light evening breeze, and floodlights illuminated the area where investigators had swarmed earlier. Now, it was empty. Despite the warm weather he felt a chill pass through him. Probably it was the sweat drenched shirt against the evening chill.

He started walking slowly toward the Assembly Building. He stopped a few yards short of the caution tape, his eyes surveying the grand structure that had witnessed unspeakable horrors just today. His gaze narrowed, as if he was not looking at this crime scene at all, but another one years ago, in another place, another time. A mistake that had cost lives. A mistake that was his to own.

His phone buzzed, breaking his reverie. It was a message from an unknown number, but he knew it by heart. He did not open it. Not yet.

Ajay's Internal Monologue: I could not afford to fail this time. Not again. But could I trust myself? Could I trust my team? What if—

Suddenly, he clenched his fists, eyes closed tightly, as if willing away his own thoughts.

When he opened his eyes, they were focused, the softness replaced by a steely resolve. He took a deep breath and turned away, heading back to his car. As he opened the door and sat down, he finally checked his phone. "Urgent: Let's meet tomorrow at the same place same time," the message read.

Ajay: (muttering to himself as he started the car) Okay, let us do this.

As he drove away, the Assembly Building shrank in his rear-view mirror, but the weight it added was something he knew he would carry forward. For better or worse, it was a part of him now.

His phone buzzed again, another message, another responsibility, another chance to make things right. And with that thought, he accelerated into the thickening night.

At the police headquarters, things were in full swing in the Bomb Squad wing. The team that had collected evidence at the explosion site was busy numbering and cataloguing the various items they had brought back. Sohail felt that one of the pieces looked familiar. It was a portion of a microchip, with some alphabets and a logo visible on it. He was pretty sure that he had seen something similar if not exactly same. He wanted to compare it with the database, but first everything needed to be processed.

Sohail did not say anything to anyone but one of the members doing the numbering realised something was bugging him. Sohail hovered around their desk without saying anything, but it felt as if he was dying to get his hands on the database as soon as the processing was over. One of the cataloguers asked Sohail if he wanted anything but Sohail denied, attributing his restlessness to the start of a new investigation.

The processing of each piece of evidence collected was a meticulous and time-consuming process. Each pouch had to be numbered first. Then, the photographer took a photo of the evidence still inside the plastic pouch. This photo was to be used during investigation as well as exhibit if the matter reached the courts. After this, all the evidence numbers were entered on a file with detailed description. The description included details like size, material, where it was found, who had found it, etc. The person making the list could also write his or her comments/ observations. Other team members also got a chance to add to this column later. The idea was to have so exhaustive an information about the evidence on paper that there was no need to handle the evidence itself in course of the investigation. Of course, if an expert wanted to examine it that would be surely allowed. The detailed description could then be fed into the database for future reference. This method enabled collection of information from every possible source, which came in handy when the team went through everything meticulously.

Ideally everyone should have contributed to the description before going off. There was every chance of forgetting some minor detail with time. But it was getting so late that there was no point in asking everyone to wait. If they left late, there would be delay in the morning. It was more important to start working on it immediately first thing in the morning. Satyarthi repeated as much to all his team members when they came to him to take leave. Except the photographer and two people involved in numbering, everyone else including Sohail went home. There was nothing to be done before processing was complete and it would take majority part of the night to get it done.

It was almost two in the morning when everything was finished. All the pieces of evidence were put in a carton and locked away. It was more precious than any gems and jewellery that any lady would have owned in the world!!

31-01-2018

Satyarthi was the last person to leave the night before but was already in his seat when the team started trickling in the next morning. The first one to turn up was Sohail. He went to the case room immediately and started looking at the register. Then he realised that he must have the evidence number to look at its description. He went straight to Satyarthi's room and asked for the photographs. Satyarthi was also looking at the photographs. They both went through them silently again and again. Then Sohail extracted one of the photos and said that he felt he had seen a similar item elsewhere recently. This made Satyarthi leap with joy because if this hunch was correct, they could be on to something immediately. He asked Sohail to start looking into the database without any delay.

Looking up photos was no big joke. Each case has hundreds of photographs associated with it. Even two years ago it would have been an almost impossible task. However, all the records were now computerised and hence much easier to look up.

Sohail logged into the system immediately and went about his job expertly. He scanned the photo and set up an image search in the database. He was not expecting much from the first search but started it nonetheless because it felt good to start. It was highly unlikely that the search would give an image 80% match. Sohail was proved right exactly 7 minutes and 32 seconds later. When the search threw up an empty result.

He started setting up another search, which would bring up images that partially matched. As this would take a much longer time, Sohail went off in search of tea. Many more of his colleagues had turned up by this time. He had also gained a partner in the form of Raghav. Raghav had joined the force only a couple of years ago. But he had showed promise in many of the cases due to his eye for detail and strong deductive logic. That Satyarthi had assigned him Raghav meant they were expected to come up with positive results. Also, it implied that Satyarthi had no better lead to follow. By the time Sohail came back from his tea break, Raghav had already taken command of the console and stared at it intently. But the staring did nothing to speed up the process. The search was only 50%

complete. The more time search took, more the number of images that would come up.

However, Sohail was not sure whether he should be happy about it because sieving through the images would take that much longer time. Raghav was of the opposite opinion. True that it would take more time but it would also increase the probability of finding the photo Sohail had seen earlier. Their discussion and postulations continued another 25 minutes before the result was ready. More than 4000 images had come up. They started the sorting with cases on which Sohail had worked. It was more likely that he had seen it on one of his own cases. Then Raghav made a few more adjustments and they started looking at the images one by one. Both were sitting on different computers to expedite the process. A huge screen in front of them showed a blow up of the evidence whose match they were trying to locate. If they failed to find a match, they would have to go through manufacturer database. If there was a match, they were hoping that they will not have to hunt for the information again.

It took them better part of the day to find the image about which Sohail could have been talking. It was an exhibit from the police headquarter bombing the previous year. It was not an exact match but the number on both seemed to be part of the same number printed by the manufacturer!

CHAPTER 5

01/04/2017 (10 months ago)

Matching of evidence with that of Police Headquarter bombing last year had a mixed effect on Satyarthi. At once he was relieved to find at least something to work upon but also something shook within him as he was reminded of that fateful day. He was present there and had seen his colleagues dying with his own eyes.

It started like any other day at the police headquarters. The new wing for Pink Patrol was to be inaugurated by the Chief Minister at 12:30. The Pink Patrol wing inauguration was a significant event, given the rising cases of violence against women in the city. This new wing had been added to ensure privacy for female police staff as well complainants. As it was the headquarters, many women turned up regularly to report crimes against them but felt uncomfortable reporting to male policemen. The new wing had been started as a confidence building measure among the common people for the police force.

The atmosphere was solemn and heavy with apprehension. Traditionally Indian Police has been a male bastion and continues to be so even in the third decade of 21st century. Women constitute just over 11% of the police forces. So, all the male officers and constables were wary. But enthusiastic as well, ready to embrace the new beginnings.

Everybody turned up in time, looking sharp in their uniform. The police commissioner Mr. Kaale also arrived at 9:00 a.m. Maybe that was the reason that everyone was so punctual and alert. All the preparations for the inauguration had been completed the day before but still last moment touches were being put everywhere.

Satyarthi was working away in the bomb squad room with 2 of his colleagues working on a report about a series of bombings that had recently gripped the CM's constituency. As the chief minister was coming for the inauguration, he expected him to ask about the progress. The case involved explosion at the heart of an industrial hub, supposedly by some terrorist groups who wanted to put across their point. Like other incidents it was a long shot that anything would come out of this investigation so soon. As the place was 60 kilometres away, they had taken more than a couple of hours in reaching the site. Despite the local police having cordoned off the area, as it was in the open, they expected lots of evidence to have either disappeared or got contaminated. But that was work and you could always expect the chief minister to remember the cases and ask about their progress. That's why the three men were putting together a report.

The Chief Minister arrived in time at exactly 12:25. Unlike other politicians, he was always known to be punctual for all his appointments. Even after becoming the chief minister. He was accompanied by his secretary, Naveen, the Home Minister, and his bodyguards. He never travelled with a large cavalcade. He treated it as waste of money, resources, time. This was easy on the organisers as well because they had that many less people to host.

The Pink Patrol wing was inaugurated in time and then the chief minister with his secretary and home minister assembled in the commissioner's office for snacks and a cup of tea. After the initial small talk, the Commissioner updated Shantanu about progress made in various high-profile cases the CM had shown interest in. As expected, Satyarthi was called in to present his report. He briefed the chief minister and then also handed over the report to his secretary. Satyarthi was courteous but very brief and to the point. Never one to make much small talk with anyone. This had also ensured that none of his bosses felt threatened by his ways and hence placed immense trust in him.

After the Chief Minister left around 1:30, everyone got back to their regular routine. The Commissioner Mr Kaale himself had many files to take care of and he spent the next hour working through the pile. He was thankful that in this hot Indian summer the crimes were a little less and there was some breathing space. Also, it was quite challenging for his team to commute in the scorching heat and collect evidence, talk to witnesses and co-ordinate with other government agencies when most of them were preparing to go on a summer holiday.

Satyarthi was locked up in the case room with his colleagues, the walls covered with maps, timelines and surveillance photos. As the clock struck 3:00 p.m., a muffled boom reverberated through the building, rattling windows and shaking the floor beneath them. For a split second, time seemed to freeze. Satyarthi's eyes widened, his body tensed, every muscle ready to respond to the emergency that was unfolding. Because he did not need to be told that it was a bomb that had exploded very near him.

Within a few seconds came a secondary explosion, louder and more devastating than the first, its impact resonating through the building's foundation like a shockwave. Satyarthi was already on his feet, his chair falling backward with a clatter as he sprinted out of his office. The corridor was a labyrinth of chaos; officers were staggering out of their rooms, some rushing forward, others frantically calling out for help or trying to assemble teams to manage the crisis. But Satyarthi had only one focus: getting to the source of the explosions, knowing that every second could mean the difference between life and death for the people caught in the blasts.

When he reached the site of the first explosion, he felt his stomach tighten. The Commissioner's car had been reduced to a smoking hulk of twisted metal. Body parts and debris were scattered in a grotesque radius around the vehicle. The flames from the second explosion engulfed the walls of the toilet block, where the ceiling had caved in. He held onto the pillar beside him to steady himself. And then a third one exploded right in front of his eyes, deafening and disorienting, filling the air with thick, black smoke and the smell of burning metal and rubber. Amidst the score of policemen gathered to have a cup of tea to refresh themselves.

Later, the body count was put to 20. And there were more than 40 injured admitted to the nearby hospitals. It also included some civilians who had come in to ask about their cases or simply get a glimpse of the chief minister. It seemed as if their death had stopped them from going; after all, it had been almost two hours since he had gone away.

There was complete mayhem in front of Satyarthi's eyes. Most of the onlookers were too shocked to react.

When an emergency happens, people call the police. Whom do the police call when an emergency strikes them?

Though not the senior officer on site, Satyarthi was acutely aware of the urgent need to preserve evidence at the blast sites. He quickly found the highest-ranking officer amidst the chaos and insisted on immediate cordoning off of the affected areas. Navigating through the pandemonium, he began placing markers and directing his squad to isolate the zones where the blasts had occurred. As a Bomb Squad leader, he knew that the integrity of these sites could provide crucial leads to those responsible for this horrific act.

But as he worked, he felt an internal tug at his emotions. These were not just coordinates on a map or abstract locations; they were intimate spaces in his daily life that had been violated. He had sat in the Commissioner's car during discussions on many cases. He had used that toilet block, and he had taken breaks in that now-destroyed canteen. As he looked at the wreckage and the faces of his colleagues—some wounded, some dazed, and some missing—he felt shattered. These were not just scenes of professional interest; they were personal tragedies inscribed in places he had once found ordinary, even comforting. And now they stood as twisted landscapes, bearing the marks of unfathomable violence and loss.

The initial casualty count was devastating: 20 dead, over 40 injured. And though the numbers would be revised in the days to come, for Satyarthi, they were already too high. His face became a mask, his emotions locked behind a wall of professional duty. But deep within, a storm was brewing, a hurricane of questions, doubts and a newly kindled fire to find those responsible.

During investigation, it was found that around 3 o'clock, Mr. Kaale had received a phone call and he started out immediately. His driver was waiting at the bottom of the steps. He started to come out to open the door but he signalled him not to bother. The moment he opened the door of the car a bomb exploded, tearing him to smithereens. There were two more blasts within a few seconds in the compound — one in the toilet and another in front of the canteen.

Everyone assumed that as the police headquarters housed the offices of the local Bomb Squad, and the collection of evidence started immediately, breakthrough would be achieved quickly. But that was not so, though not for lack of effort. Besides ensuring there was minimum contamination of physical evidence, Satyarthi did not let the uninjured civilians go before interviewing them.

The investigation was conducted in full swing after that but effectively it had not come to much. Despite all the pressures being added by all possible quarters — politicians, media and common people. The common narrative in media and elsewhere was the same: how could people place their trust in the hands of Police if they could not safeguard their own bastion.

And this was the nightmare Satyarthi had been reminded of now. Satyarthi could not escape the sinking feeling that washed over him as he reviewed the evidence collect till now. Just ten months had passed since the bombing at the police headquarters, but the details now before him made him realise this was not just another case. The striking similarities between the two cases could not be a mere coincidence. The one major similarity was that both could have caused much more deaths but seemed to be designed for minimum casualties. It unsettled him that Assembly bombing seemed like a grim continuation of the Police HQ bombings.

He wondered: If these two cases were connected, what did that say about the investigation into the first bombing? Had they overlooked something crucial? The notion that the past tragedy could have been averted—or that its perpetrators could have been caught sooner—loomed as a haunting possibility. With that haunting thought, Satyarthi knew he had to reconcile his inner turmoil and ensure it did not hinder his role in this crucial investigation. The stakes were already painfully high; they became personal now.

Satyarthi debated whether he should call Ajay immediately or study the files before informing him. But just then he heard a jeep stopping outside with a screech. Something told him that it must be Ajay, and yes, soon enough he could hear his casual and loud banter from outside. Satyarthi was irked because he himself was serious by nature, talked to others only when required and only whatever was required, and normally did not approve of people who were so much at ease with themselves and those around them. It could not escape him that there was a time when he liked Ajay. But he quickly drove that feeling out of his mind and waited impatiently for Ajay to come in. Soon enough he did.

The moment Ajay was inside Satyarthi's office, he was his professional self. He greeted Satyarthi, seated himself on the chair in front of him and asked if there had been any breakthrough although it was a bit early. Satyarthi was, in some ways, relieved to share that they had found a piece of evidence matching with that found at the site of Police HQ bombings. Ajay shot his head up from the file on which he was concentrating, because he was aware that Satyarthi was a witness to the bombing and was vital in organising the investigation and relief that followed immediately after. He was probably the investigating officer as well. He wasn't sure. But there was one thing he was sure of — Satyarthi would be dealing with this case with greater zeal and more personally after this. One could never forget the colleagues who had succumbed in front of your own eyes and that too without any fault or involvement of their own.

Satyarthi asked for Police HQ bombing files to be brought to him. He was aware of most of the details but wanted to be up to date about anything that might have been added later. It took him more than an hour to go over the file. Meanwhile Ajay had simply logged into his official account and brought up the case history on his screen. Satyarthi had seen this from the corner of his eyes and felt the need to get more comfortable with his computer soon. Yesterday he was witness to the ease with which Sohail handled the system deftly, and today, Ajay. As Ajay scrolled through the details, he felt his spirit going down because he could see that it was all pointing to nothing. There was nothing concrete to go on, there were no undercurrents that the Police usually get before big cases or any mention of information from the usual reliable sources.

When he finished, Ajay looked at Satyarthi with frustration because there was not much to go on from the case history. Except may be following up on the suspects.

Which they decided to do. Since Satyarthi's current team had a few people who had worked on the old case, he volunteered for the follow ups. Ajay was grateful for it because his team was already overworked collating and following up on the testimonies they had collected. Satyarthi called Sohail and asked him to find the latest whereabouts of the eight people who had been arrested in connection with the police headquarter bombings. He also asked him to give a status update every 2 hours.

As Ajay was coming out Sonia reached there with her camera setup. She had come to report on the latest development in the Assembly bombing case. She had been to the Assembly earlier in the day, but could not find much to report. There were just a handful of policemen around, guarding the place. So, she made a move to the Police HQ. Since the bomb squad was stationed there, she hoped to get at least some soundbites for her news channel.

She felt it was lucky to have got hold of the investigating officer in charge. She could not know the internal arrangement that it was Satyarthi who was supposed to be talking with the media. She thrust the mic in front of Ajay and started questioning him rapidly.

Sonia: "What is the latest update in the Assembly bombing case? Have any arrests been made?"

Ajay: "It is still too early to say anything. We are investigating every possible angle."

Sonia: "Last year this headquarter was bombed and now the Assembly. Can you tell me why the police are not able to do anything? We would have expected the police to be more alert after their own headquarters were attacked."

Ajay: (irritation showing clearly on his face) "See madam, we are doing our work and we are alert to what is happening around us. It is not that we want......."

Just then Ajay felt a hand pressing down his shoulder and turned around to see Satyarthi standing there. Someone must have informed him that some journalists had arrived and Ajay was speaking to them. Ajay was grateful for the intervention, for he could feel he was going to utter something he should not, that too in front of live camera rolling.

Satyarthi faced Sonali, asking her to direct her questions to him.

Satyarthi: (After listening intently) "We are also deeply agitated by the Assembly bombing and trying our best to catch the culprits as soon as possible. We cannot let those who attacked the symbol of democracy get away."

Sonia: "First police headquarters and now the Assembly. What next can we expect?"

Satyarthi: "Please do not forget that we lost 20 of our men in the police headquarter bombing and we are grateful that there has been no casualty in the Assembly. I can assure you that there will be no further such cases."

Sonia: (with sarcasm dripping from her voice) "You are the head of Bomb Squad of the police, right? Do you get active only after an explosion has occurred?"

Satyarthi: (in a chilling tone) "You got the first part correct Madam. Our duty is to collect evidence and investigate the case based on that. Please rest assured that we are doing our best in the case."

With this, Satyarthi turned around, signalling the end on conversation. But Sonali could sense from his darkening eyes and icy tone that mentioning the Police HQ bombings had rankled something in Satyarthi. Another piece of observation filed away for use later.

Ajay had been watching on the side-lines as the mild mannered and introvert Satyarthi spoke so eloquently to the journalist. Ajay had always admired Satyarthi's calm but firm demeanour; he was grateful he had pulled him out of a potential landmine once again.

Ajay also turned and followed in his footsteps so as not to be apprehended by the reporter again. Sonia tried to call after him but he waved her off. She shouted, "don't forget to watch my coverage on TV in the evening."

It was very late at night that Ajay reached home and turned on the TV. He had spent his whole day going through the interviews of the legislators. There had not been much because everybody had come and gone straight away to the Assembly Hall for the Martyr's Day. Everybody's version was almost the same. They had waited for the Chief Minister so that the function could begin. They had no idea what to expect and hence there was some frustration as well as anticipation.

It is not that Ajay was hoping to find much information but still he went through all in case she could find something. Investigation was like that — looking for the proverbial needle in the haystack. Once you found the needle all the effort proved worthwhile.

CHAPTER 6

03-02-2018

Four days after the bombing, Sonia was again on the scene, microphone in hand, documenting the unfolding aftermath. As a seasoned crime journalist, she had covered numerous stories, but this hit close to home. She had not yet come to terms with the fact that some terrorist group had the audacity to desecrate the temple of democracy.

"I stand here less than a week after the tragic bombing at the assembly hall, a place meant for public discourse and democracy," she narrated live on her news channel. "The echoes of last year's police headquarters bombing reverberate through this tragedy, raising questions that are uncomfortable yet essential: Can our law enforcement agencies protect us? Can they even protect themselves?"

It was a Saturday and the police stations were unofficially in a weekend mood. Ajay personally turned up at his police station every Saturday because he anyways did not have much to do at home. Being at home was either lonely or almost always ended in a fight when his mother was in town. He used work as his excuse to fill the Saturdays.

Today he had also called Satyarthi for a meeting. In fact, it was Satyarthi's suggestion because he did not want to go to his own office, where there would be so many other things taking up his time. Usually Saturday was for taking stock of progress made on different cases through the week. But right now, with the Commissioner and the CM's office breathing down their necks, Satyarthi did not want to distract himself.

Ajay's Police station was nearer to Satyarthi's home and hence easier for him to go as well. Satyarthi updated Ajay on the progress made in the investigation.

After hitting a dead end with the police headquarters bombing file, Satyarthi had assigned Sohail to investigate the peculiar logo and number (which seemed to be part of some serial number) found etched onto the fragment of the bomb. Though information gained via the dark web was not officially admissible, Sohail had used his substantial expertise in navigating to gather invaluable intel. He had compiled a list of potential suppliers who might have provided the materials for the bomb, but the tricky part was converting this clandestine information into something they could use in an official investigation.

Legally, they could not just storm into a place based on a dark web tip; they needed concrete proof. So, Sohail was employing an alternative strategy. He was engaging these suppliers under a pseudonym, attempting to enter negotiations for sample materials. It was a risky gambit. On one hand, these were criminals who might suspect a trap; on the other, it was their best shot at getting traceable evidence. If they could just get one of these suppliers to send a sample, they could leverage their police resources to trace the package's origin. Suppliers rarely included return addresses on such shipments for obvious reasons, but the police had their ways of tracing a parcel's journey across the country.

The plan was fraught with challenges, both ethical and procedural. Satyarthi was acutely aware that they were walking a fine line, but the stakes were too high to be bound by conventional approaches. The chilling similarities between the assembly bombing and the one at the police headquarters just 10 months ago left no room for caution. Time was of the essence, and they had to act swiftly before the perpetrators struck again. If they could strike twice in a span of 10 months, they very well could again. They seemed to be on a mission of their own. It was not just about catching the criminals; it was about restoring a damaged trust between the public and the police, a trust further shaken with each passing day and each critical news report.

Satyarthi was not only grappling with the immediate logistical challenges but also the haunting echoes of the past. Every lead that ended up being a dead end and every pressurising media report from journalists like Sonia was a stark reminder of the bombing at the place he had considered a second home. This case was not just another file on his desk; it was personal.

Ajay was also becoming increasingly frustrated with the lack of tangible leads. He had been painstakingly going through interviews with legislators about their movements on the morning of the bombing. To make matters worse, not all the CCTV cameras were functioning properly at the time of the incident, offering him only fragmented visuals. In a parallel effort, he had tasked two constables with reviewing a week's worth of CCTV footage from the Assembly complex. Even though the Assembly was in session during that time, severely limiting unauthorized access, Ajay felt compelled to leave no stone unturned.

The assembly hall was a hive of activity with legislators, custodial staff, security personnel, canteen workers, library staff and even the librarian herself frequenting the area. This ballooned the list of potential suspects to nearly 200 individuals, making the investigation a daunting task. The one oddity that had emerged was an incident involving a peon who had struggled to unlock the assembly hall on the morning of the bombing. Ajay mulled over whether this minor hiccup could be a clue pointing to tampering with the lock.

Two other details from the file caught Ajay's attention. First, the CCTV system underwent a daily 15-minute shutdown at 1:00 AM for maintenance. Second, there was a documented power outage on January 29th from approximately 3:00 to 4:00 PM. During these times, all the cameras had failed to record any activity. Intriguingly, the contractor responsible for maintaining the electrical system had taken an unusually long time to address the outage, even though preparations for an important session were underway. Ajay had noted this lapse for further investigation and decided to talk to the contractor himself.

After discussing these facts with Satyarthi, both officers agreed that the bombs could likely have been planted either during the power outage in the afternoon or during the late-night maintenance window. Night security staff are usually more vigilant because of the perception that nighttime is a vulnerable period, but Satyarthi and Ajay considered that professional criminals might think differently. During the day, the hustle and bustle could offer a camouflage, making it easier for someone to plant the bomb. If discovered, the perpetrator could use the crowd as a diversion, making their escape more feasible.

This led them to a single conclusion: the electrical outage was probably no accident but a calculated move by the individuals plotting to plant the bomb. This underscored the likelihood that the event was an inside job, adding another layer of complexity and urgency to an already intricate investigation.

Just as Ajay and Satyarthi were discussing the case, Satyarthi's sister Kusum entered with a tiffin box in her hands. As soon as Kusum opened the door Ajay turned around to see who had disturbed them and their eyes met. Both froze for a couple of seconds. Kusum was the first one to recover and moved towards Satyarthi, saying she had brought his tiffin that he had forgotten in a hurry. For a moment Satyarthi was also taken aback on seeing her but he also composed himself immediately. He also realised that he will have questions to answer when he went home tonight. Especially from his wife.

Not knowing what to do, Ajay flipped open his mobile, extracted the number of his contact at the Assembly and rang him up. By the time he was done, Kusum would have left and the embarrassing situation would have ceased to exist.

Ajay did not spend more than 10 minutes on the phone but by the time he had finished he had forgotten all about Kusum's appearance. There was a sparkle in his eyes as he felt he was onto something. During the electrical breakdown on 29th, the Chief Minister was also present. The contractor had been informed of the problem by the librarian as she was there in the Chief Minister's office when this had happened. The Chief Minister himself had instructed the librarian to inform the contractor immediately.

Ajay next called up the contractor's office, introduced himself and asked to speak to the person responsible for attending to the Assembly electrical maintenance. When the concerned person came on phone, Ajay asked him what the trouble was.

Contractor — "sir, it was a minor short circuit which we could correct immediately."

Ajay — "then why had if taken more than an hour to restore the power."

Contractor — "our electrician took 20 minutes to reach the assembly and he did the work in 10 minutes. Sir, we did it within 30 minutes of being informed."

Ajay — "can you tell me the exact time when you had received the complain?"

Contractor – "yes sir please let me look in the complaint register. (After a couple of minutes) according to our register the complaint was made at 3:40."

Ajay called back his contact at the assembly and asked to be connected to the librarian. He was informed that the library was closed on Saturdays and hence the librarian was also not there. Ajay thanked him and put the phone down.

Ajay then opened the interview file and looked for the librarian's statement but he could not find it. He called Karuna at the police station and asked her why the librarian's sheet was not there in the file. She told him that the librarian might have been absent that day. She asked Ajay to hold while she checked the list. The librarian was there on the employee list but absent on 30th.

Letting out a slow whistle, Ajay turned towards Satyarthi. During all these phone calls and discussions

Satyarthi had listened quietly. He knew it would be best not to disturb Ajay while he was on a roll. He would draw him in when he felt he had something concrete to share. Ajay filled him in with details he must not have heard from the other side of the telephone, though he could have guessed easily.

The librarian had delayed informing the electrical maintenance company. The question was, why. Was it because she was busy with the CM or there was something else at play.

11-02-18

It was after a long time that Shantanu had got a Sunday that was relatively free. He did not have anything on schedule after the weekly morning meeting with the people. Since assuming office, Shantanu had shifted the weekly people's meeting from Thursdays to Sunday; he felt more people would be able to come on a Sunday rather than a weekday. It was the usual lot of people complaining about lack of amenities, wanting jobs, help for educating their kids or financial grant for their NGOs. By 10 o'clock Shantanu was free. He had also delegated the necessary actions to be taken. He was considering spending the afternoon with his daughter because she often complained that he had no time for her, when one of the guards came running to him. It was very uncharacteristic of him to do so because the security guards were usually equanimous people who hardly showed any emotions or disruptive behaviour. For a moment he got worried but soon enough the guard came up to him and told him that his mentor was at the gates and coming up in a very foul mood without waiting for completing the formalities at the gate.

This was not the way it had ever happened. He was usually a calm and quiet person who followed the rules without any complain. He had had enough of flouting the rules in his youth.

And sure enough, Shantanu saw Rajan Chaudhari coming up to him with rapid strides. He got up immediately from his seat and rushed towards him with folded hands. Before he could greet him, Rajan waved him off with a wave of his hand and proceeded uninvited towards the home office. He knew the ins and outs of the CM bungalow as he was a frequent visitor as well as an astute observer. Even in this stressful situation Shantanu could not help but smile to himself because Naveen was working inside the office and he had no idea that Rajan was coming up in such a foul mood. As it was, Naveen had never warmed up to him and always looked at him with suspicion. But then, he was so devoted to Shantanu that he looked with suspicion at anyone who came close.

The moment the door was closed behind them, Rajan exploded and started shouting like a maniac — have you grown up so much that you can take such important decisions on your own without consulting me? Have you forgotten the day when you had just landed here and did not have the wherewithal to get two square meals a day? If I had not taken you under my wings, you might have starved to death or beaten up by your so-called friends to pulp.

Naveen, who was working in the inner office, went out the door on listening all this because he knew his boss would want to have this conversation in private. It was not clear if Rajan had noticed that Naveen was also present and had heard whatever he had said. It was not clear from

Naveen's facial expression if those statements had raised any questions in his mind.

Rajan said again — how could you take such an important decision about the farmers of your constituency without consulting with me? Have you forgotten that it was me who had proposed the idea of taking up the farmers' movement and building your political base from there? Because you understand farmers and their woes. Whichever part of the country they belonged to. But do you think you have started understanding what they want better, now that you are the chief minister?

Rajan ranted on and on as Shantanu quietly listened to everything he had to say. It is not that he could not counter whatever was said but he waited for the steam to dissipate before saying anything. Otherwise, it would have been as useless as banging your head against the concrete wall.

Just then the house help came in with a tray of tea and snacks sent by Maitreyi. Shantanu was thankful for this interruption. Someone must have informed her that Rajan had come in a very foul mood because he could see some of his favourite snacks sitting beside the teapot. It did not miss even Rajan and he remained quiet till the tea was being poured and served. Suddenly he remembered the times when Shantanu was an upcoming politician and Rajan would drop into their home often late at night after a hard day's work. Maitreyi would always be ready with simple but delicious dinner; never complaining. Those thoughts and images made him even more angry rather than mellowing down. He felt that Shantanu was destroying all the hard work that had been put into the rise of his career by everyone around him, including his wife.

Someone who had stood by him through thick and thin, never complaining about being the breadwinner as well as caretaker of the family when Shantanu had no time or money for these domestic matters.

The tea break made Rajan Chaudhari more sensible to where he was and what he was saying, though not necessarily less angry. He resumed his tirade after finishing his tea!

Meanwhile Naveen paced the lawns in front of the office restlessly. He had been with Shantanu since his farmer agitation days in college but he had not seen Rajan Chaudhari so angry ever. He felt more than a bit scared.

It was more than an hour when Rajan Chaudhari finally came out of the CM office. Naveen went inside to find the chief minister sitting back in a pensive mood in his chair, eyes closed and fingers tapping a pencil on the desk in front of him. His posture told Naveen he did not want to be disturbed and waited patiently for him to come out of his reverie.

It was some minutes before Shantanu opened his eyes to find Naveen sitting calmly in front of him. He often wondered, especially at times like these, what he would have done without Naveen. Naveen had been with him since his college days, rather their college days because they were in the same college and part of the same Students Union. He guiltily remembered that Maitreyi was also a part of their gang but she had so quietly taken to domesticity after their marriage. She quickly realised that if they wanted the marriage to work, one of them would have to sacrifice their ambitions. Whatever doubts she had in her mind simply vanished after their son was born. She knew that being the mother she will have to take charge of the house. Because anyone can be the breadwinner or the provider of the family but not a mother.

After a couple of minutes staring at Naveen, Shantanu let out his breath; it seemed he had been holding it for long. Whatever it was, he could not share with Naveen. He got on with routine work because now he was in no mood to play with his daughter. He felt it would be better if he at least caught up with some work rather than wasting away the time thinking about what all his mentor had said.

When Naveen tried to ask him about Rajan, he just said, "Oh, nothing, *Godom* was angry. I will manage. Tell Maitreyi to invite him for dinner sometime next week."

20-02-2018

Around 9:30 AM

Rajan Chaudhari sat in the backseat of his bulletproof car, en route to the temple — his unwavering weekly ritual whenever he was in the city. Despite the captivating beauty of the day, the weight of something undefined marred his spirits. His weathered eyes stared out the window but saw nothing, lost in a sea of contemplation.

Abruptly, the driver slammed on the brakes, jolting Rajan forward, colliding him against the back of the driver's seat. Though uninjured, his heart rate spiked. Irritated, he was about to chastise the driver when he noticed the crowd blocking their path. An accident had occurred; a collision between two scooties, it seemed. Pedestrians had swarmed the scene — some offering help, others recording the incident on their phones.

"Check what's happening," Rajan ordered his driver, who returned after a brief inspection. "Three to four minutes, sir. They'll clear out."

Just then, a knock on the window diverted his attention — a young beggar boy, palm outstretched, eyes filled with a mixture of desperation and hope. Normally, Rajan might have ignored such an interruption, but on his way to the temple, he had a policy to never refuse anyone asking for alms. Reaching into his pocket, he retrieved a 10 rupee note and rolled down the window.

As his hand moved towards the window, time seemed to slow. Out of nowhere, a motorbike roared up alongside his car. Two men, garbed head-to-toe in black with masks concealing their faces, emerged like specters. Without a moment's hesitation, they opened fire. Bullets ripped through the air, piercing Rajan's chest and shoulders, shattering the illusion of his bulletproof existence.

Chaos erupted. People screamed and scattered in every direction. Car tires screeched as drivers slammed their brakes, narrowly avoiding the panicked crowd. The motorbike sped away, its riders vanishing as quickly and mysteriously as they had appeared.

Inside the car, the driver sat paralysed by a blend of shock and fear, his hands trembling on the wheel. Outside, the beggar boy who had knocked on Rajan's window looked on, the 10 rupee note still clutched in his hand. And then, as if his reverie had been shattered, he ran and melted in the crowd.

Within moments, although it felt like an eternity, someone finally found the presence of mind to call the police. The crowd that was gathered in front of the car just a few moments ago now surrounded the car. And as the sirens wailed in the distance, coming ever closer, everyone knew that they would arrive too late to save Rajan Chaudhari, a man both powerful and now, tragically, powerless.

When Ajay arrived at the crime scene, navigating through the suffocating traffic congestion was a challenge. A sense of urgency filled the air; he had to act swiftly to control the situation and preserve evidence. Ajay wasted no time. He dispatched four constables, sending two in each direction, with strict instructions to reverse the traffic flow and alleviate the jam.

Grabbing the loudspeaker, he addressed the crowd. "Please remain calm and cooperate with the police. Stay where you are. We need your assistance." By then, word had spread on social media about Rajan Chaudhari's identity. Although Ajay knew this would escalate public interest, his immediate concern was the crime scene. Ajay radioed for the forensic team to arrive ASAP while directing his own team to start preserving evidence for them to analyse. He also alerted the social media cell to monitor any potentially useful or disruptive online conversations.

Aware of Chaudhari's significant influence, Ajay knew the case would attract massive attention and pressure from the public and media. But these were concerns for later; his immediate focus was the integrity of the crime scene and the gathering of evidence.

Methodical as ever, Ajay quickly drafted a concise questionnaire for interviewing witnesses. He instructed Karuna to team up with another constable and start speaking with the crowd, emphasizing the need for a soft, polite approach given the heightened emotions and frustrations caused by the delays. Considering it was the early morning traffic, everyone was on their way to office, and delays meant repercussions for them.

Turning his attention back to the immediate vicinity, he assigned constables to cordon off the crime scene to prevent any inadvertent tampering. Then he guided Rajan Chaudhari's trembling driver to his own police jeep for a private interview. "You're our most critical witness," Ajay told him softly, "and I need you to be clear-headed when recounting what happened." The driver began his account, pausing occasionally, his voice tinged with nervous energy. Ajay handed him water from his own flask to calm his nerves. "Take your time," he encouraged, "every detail counts."

As he listened, Ajay knew that every minute piece of information would be critical. The driver's account, the witness testimonies, the background chatter on social media — each component was a piece of a jigsaw puzzle that Ajay was determined to solve. And solving it started with focusing on the here and now, ensuring every detail was meticulously recorded and analysed.

After hearing the driver's story, the first thing Ajay did was to order a constable to locate and bring the two individuals involved in the earlier scootie collision to him immediately.

After the driver had completed his story, Ajay asked him more questions. Just to cross-check nothing had been omitted the first time. Sometimes new crucial details that were missed in the first narration come up the second time. He also dispatched another constable to see if there were any beggar boys around. He felt it was too much of a coincidence that the boy forced Rajan Chaudhari to roll down the window to provide the killers an opportune moment.

Ajay dismissed the driver after taking down his address and mobile number. With the instruction to not leave the city without intimating him and that he could be called to the police station for further enquiries, if required. The two constables returned to recount that two girls were driving the scooties that had collided, and neither the girls not any beggar boy was to be found. The two girls seemed to have silently slipped off when the police came. Since they were on their own vehicle, it could be easily inferred that they moved off the moment they heard the siren. When others around them were concentrating on the police and waiting for their arrival, they made their escape. And yes, it was an escape because it was clear even to a novice that the whole charade had been played out to ensure that the car of Rajan Chaudhari would stop. This also meant that the beggar boy was also a plant by the killers to expose Rajan Chaudhari.

Meanwhile the forensic team and ambulance rolled up to the scene and started about their tasks with precision and urgency. First on their agenda seemed to be documenting the bullet trajectory and impact points on Rajan Chaudhari's bulletproof car. The technicians took photographs from multiple angles, marked the bullet holes and collected any stray bullet casings that had landed on the vehicle or nearby.

Next, they carefully approached the body of Rajan Chaudhari. Donning gloves, they combed through his clothes for gunpowder residue and other trace evidence that might offer clues about the gunmen. After all, the killers had fired from almost point-blank range. They also took swabs for DNA analysis and bagged his personal items, including his wallet and phone, preserving them for further examination. Once these initial steps were done, the body was respectfully lifted onto a stretcher and transported to the hospital for an autopsy.

Then came the task of thoroughly combing the surrounding area. Technicians scoured the pavement and the nearby foliage, meticulously picking up anything that looked out of the ordinary: fibres, shards of glass or unidentifiable substances that might yield chemical traces of the assailants. A 3D laser scanner was used to capture the entire scene, providing an invaluable tool for future re-examinations and reconstructions of the event.

Lastly, they focused on the crowd that had been around at the time of the shooting. Any cups, bottles or trash that could have fingerprints or DNA were bagged and tagged. Even a piece of chewing gum could serve as a crucial link to a suspect, and nothing was left to chance. The forensic team knew they were dealing with a high-profile case and did not leave anything to chance. Since the crime had been committed in the open, they knew this was their only chance to collect evidence. Soon, change in weather and continuous traffic would wipe out everything.

The team was grateful that it was still morning and that the weather was holding up. The good lighting conditions were invaluable for photography and the lack of rain meant that crucial evidence remained undisturbed. As they wrapped up their on-site work, Ajay looked at the sky and exhaled. It was a race against the setting sun, but for now, they had seized the moment, collecting what would hopefully be the essential pieces to solving this gruesome puzzle.

CHAPTER 7

20-02-2018, late afternoon

Ajay had hardly finished his cup of tea after reaching the police station when his phone rang. It was Naveen — CM's secretary. He simply said that the Chief Minister wanted to talk to him and put the CM on. The CM sounded very disturbed and emotionally shaken up. His voice was low, without its usual strength. He seemed to be speaking with supreme effort. He asked Ajay about Rajan Chaudhari's murder and if there was anything leading to the murderers. It then struck Ajay that Rajan Chaudhari was the CM's mentor. This added to his burden of having to handle a political murder case.

Whether the murder was politically inspired or not would be established later but the politicians from all quarters would be pressing for quick arrest of the people responsible. Many of them would not have met the deceased in the last couple of years or bothered whether he was dead or alive, but his death was to be encashed as much as possible by everyone. Old semi-retired politicians were usually every party's property. And especially when some mishap occurred to them, everyone thought it prudent to show solidarity with the senior member of the fraternity. Ajay had seen this play out several times in the past and could never be sure if this was out of real concern for one of their kind or just a political gimmick to remain relevant and newsworthy.

In the age of 24-hour news cycles and relentless quest for viral content, Rajan Chaudhari's murder would be a golden opportunity for these small-time and long-forgotten politicians to thrust themselves into the spotlight. These opportunists, quick to ride the coattails of a tragedy, would immediately start flooding social media and television airwaves with fiery interviews and 'exclusive' statements. Add to that mix overenthusiastic and overzealous journalists like Sonia and you had a full-fledged media episode at hand.

He could almost hear Sonia branding the murder as an absolute failure of the current administration on her channel, emphasizing that even a stalwart like Chaudhari, who had been a mentor to the Chief Minister, was not safe. The narrative would quickly escalate into heated debates on national security, law and order, and even the moral fabric of society.

Others would take a more conspiratorial route, suggesting that the murder was an inside job orchestrated to eliminate a political rival or to divert attention from some other pressing issue. For them, Chaudhari's prior influence and mentorship of the Chief Minister made for a rich tapestry of political drama that could be exploited to the hilt. In this milieu of heightened political opportunism, the tragic murder would become a tool for personal agendas, clouding the real issues and potentially hindering the investigation. Amid the din of theories and allegations, the news channels and YouTube influencers would find their ratings soaring, but at the cost of turning a grave incident into a sensationalist circus.

With all these thoughts swirling in his mind, Ajay managed to pacify the CM to some extent, or at least he felt so. After putting down the phone his headache returned, which seemed to have been receding after the strong cup of tea.

The Chief Minister's call had disrupted Ajay's chain of thoughts. Plus, he was still processing the fact that it was the CM's mentor who had been murdered in broad daylight, so he will have to move things quickly and decisively. As a plan formed in his head, he meticulously began inputting every nuance of the crime scene into his computer database. His fingers tapped over the keys with a fury that matched the train of thoughts as he tried to capture the subtleties: the exact trajectory of the bullets, the vantage point of the shooters, even the precise brand of ammunition used. Information collected through pure observation. The forensic report takes time to reach the police station. Via proper channel. So early on he had got into the habit of getting as much information as he could from right at the crime scene.

Over a decade in law enforcement had strengthened Ajay's conviction that criminals, like creatures of habit, reveal themselves through recurring patterns. Whether it was the specific time of day when a crime was committed, the kind of weapon used or even the method of getaway, serial offenders had their own signature styles, much like artists. This was not unique to the criminal underworld. Professionals in any field craft their own foolproof methodologies, continually honing them for success. In the underworld, this tendency was even more pronounced because it was a necessity. Those who failed to achieve this level of professionalism were often either eliminated by rivals or apprehended by authorities.

Once Ajay finished logging the essential details, Ajay activated the search function in the database. This was not a quick process. The software would need at least 15 to 20 minutes to scan through an immense repository of criminal records from the past decade, each file representing a web of choices, strategies and betrayals. These records were not confined to local crimes; they spanned the entire country, forming a dark mishmash of human behaviour and its transgressions. Ajay deliberately set the search parameters wide open. He wanted to compare the Chaudhari case against all crimes in the database, irrespective of geography. An intuitive hunch was gnawing at him, suggesting that the murder transcended the borders of their city or even their state. Maybe it was Rajan Chaudhari's own origins fuelling this gut feeling. Having moved to the city in his late 20s, Chaudhari must have had a previous life spent at various places, and who knew which forgotten past or scorched earth had come calling for him now? The high-stakes search initiated, Ajay leaned back and stared at the screen. Each passing second expanded the web of possibilities, each finding could either crack the case wide open or send him spiralling down another rabbit hole. He waited patiently. He knew from experience that patience was a virtue that always paid.

While Ajay was waiting for the search results, Rashmi, the CCTV analyst, approached his desk with a drawn face. "Shit," Ajay muttered under his breath. Her expression was not encouraging and Ajay braced himself for some bad news. Rashmi told him that the murder had been committed in a blind spot — an area not directly covered by the CCTV cameras placed on the road. Two cameras were only partially covering it and still some part was left out. All she could manage was footage of some scooties without pillion riders, just around the time when the police reached the crime scene. She wanted to know if she should try to get a close up and see if the numbers could be spotted. She did not have much hope from that as it would take too much time without any assurance of results.

Ajay's hunch was further confirmed that it was a meticulously planned murder. He considered her question for some time and then instructed her to break her team into two — one for spotting the registration numbers of the scooties passing through the CCTV camera and another for gathering whatever footage they could from the other two cameras of the murder scene. After Rashmi left, Ajay opened the interview file lying in front of him. It had interviews with all the people that were there on the scene of crime. As he had given a set template, he knew what to look for. In 10 minutes, he had segregated sheets of 13 people who were nearest to the crime scene, specifically in front of the car. This meant that they were very near to the site of the scooty accident as well. A few of them had mentioned the accident but many had not. But then, Ajay had no idea about the accident when he was preparing the questionnaire. So, much detail about the accident was not there. But that was about to change.

In the next hour he called up all the 13 people on the mobile number supplied by them. One of them did not pick up and another one was switched off. Ajay extracted as many details as possible from the rest of the 11 people who also happened to be witness to the road accident.

These were the details that he gathered: One scooty was black while the other was red. Each was driven by a girl. Both were coming from the same direction. The girl driving the red scooty applied sudden brakes and the black one collided with her and both fell. Both got up and started arguing. They were wearing helmets but took it off as soon as they got up from the ground. However, they had wrapped up their faces to prevent sunburn and hence their faces were not clear even after they had taken off their helmets. They were still arguing when gunshots were heard and people turned their attention towards them. None of them had any idea where or when the girls had gone. Just one of the guys had seen them going away on their scooty just after the police siren was heard. He had tried to make them wait for the police to come and then maybe they could have their problems solved as well. But they seemed to be in a hurry and said had to catch their respective offices.

Listening to what the witnesses had to say, and going by the driver's narration of events, only one conclusion seemed obvious. Collision between the scooties had been orchestrated simply to stop Rajan Chaudhari's car. The girls did not want themselves identified and hence had covered their faces with scarves. They slipped off the moment people's attention was diverted towards the murder. He called up Rashmi to tell that they must concentrate only on red and black scooties. Though, these were very common colours and Ajay was not sure how useful it might prove to be.

Then he called up one of the informers in the area and asked him to find out about a beggar boy who was working the area in the morning hours around the time the murder took place. He told him, "If you suspect someone, inform me immediately and do not let the child out of sight."

By the time Ajay finished, his computer screen was flashing results. There were more than 150 matches.

He started going through them one by one. At the end of three hours, he had nothing more than a handful of probabilities. But always an optimist, he filed it for later reference.

It was already past 8 and so Ajay decided to call it a day. Nothing was to be gained by hanging around. No results or reports would be coming in before the next day. If he hurried, he might catch some of the students before they went home from the tuition.

24-02-2018

As time elapsed, Ajay felt a strong need to talk to the CM. All research on Rajan Chaudhri's past ended at the CM's doorsteps. When he was not the CM. Not even a known politician but an obscure student union activist. A deep dive into Rajan Chaudhri's past had not revealed much. At least nothing that was not publicly available and remembered. No one knew Rajan Chaudhari well. He seemed to have created this well-designed façade around him that no one alive had been able to breach. Except the CM and his wife. Ajay shuddered at his own use of the word "alive." Who knows how many skeletons he had in his closet. When any politician's life is as pristine as Rajan Chaudhri's, policemen tend to take a gloomy view of it. May be it has got something to do with the way they are trained and the way they lead a life seeped in everyday crimes.

Although it had been more than three weeks since the Assembly bombing, Ajay could still reach the chief minister through his secretary whenever he wanted. He took out his mobile and called Naveen. He was granted a meeting with the chief minister at 3:00 in the afternoon. With the instruction to be there in time because he had to attend a farmers' meeting at 4 o'clock. Ajay felt one hour would be more than sufficient.

Ajay was thankful that the Chief Minister was a stickler for time. He was shown into his office at exactly three o'clock. And they got on to business immediately. CM also did not believe in small talk, especially when it was something of utmost seriousness.

Chief Minister: "What have you been able to find out about the murder?"

Ajay: "Sir, it is too early to say anything. I am waiting for at least a few forensic reports to come in before I can say anything concretely even to you. The forensic reports always take so much time but I used your name, I hope you do not mind my doing that, to hurry up the things. So, I hope to get the photographs and analysis of tyre marks by tomorrow. Can you please tell me all you know about Mr Chaudhari? I am asking you because you have been close to him and I cannot find anyone else who knew him so well for so long."

Ajay did not say this but thought to himself - many people say that you know about Rajan Chaudhari's life from before he turned up in the city. It is that part of his life that I am interested in, but I cannot say this directly. I would need to lead up to that point.

Shantanu remained silent for a couple of minutes as if collecting his thoughts before starting. When he began speaking, the pain that he felt at the loss of his mentor was very evident. The memories seemed to torture him but he understood the necessity of reliving those moments for the sake of bringing the people who had killed his mentor to justice. He had met Rajan Chaudhari the first time when he had come to his college during student union elections. They had struck up a conversation in that very first meeting itself. Shantanu felt that he must have impressed him in some way, because he gave him his card and asked to visit his office sometime. Shantanu had always looked up to him as a dynamic politician and hence did not let go of the chance to meet him privately. He went to his office the next week and spent quite some time — almost half the day — there. He got to see how political offices functioned for the first time. And was very excited by it. That was the day he found his calling and knew in his heart that one day he will also become a politician of the stature of his idol.

When he came back to his rooms, he thought of nothing or no one except Rajan Chaudhari and his own political career. Slowly he began spending more time at the offices of Rajan Chaudhari than in college. His close friends Naveen and Maitreyi could see where he was going. They never tried to stop him but urged with him to finish his college before plunging into politics. Under the guidance of Rajan Chaudhari, he became the president of the college student union in his final year. He had plunged himself into farmer agitation much before that.

After passing out from college Shantanu officially joined the party and begin working as grassroots worker. Everything that he had learned in politics was from him and he had given him all the guidance and knowledge willingly.

At this point the CM stopped and said: "You can find more details about our association, our campaigns, etc. yourself. It is readily available in public domain"

Ajay: "Can you think of some of his enemies, people who could want him dead?"

Chief Minister: "*Godom* had retired from active politics long back. I cannot think of anyone who would wish him dead after these many years. Someone might be nursing a grievance since his active political days; I cannot say anything about that. But still, I feel that wanting him dead would be an extreme step for a semi-retired politician."

Ajay: "With due respect Sir, what I have heard is that he had retired from active politics but was still calling the shots behind the scenes. He had retired from being the king to being the king maker."

Chief minister (a bit irritated): "Over the past couple of years, he had stopped discussing active politics with me. I would not know anything about his present engagements."

Ajay found this hard to believe. His investigations had revealed that Rajan Chaudhari was a regular visitor at the CM's residence and spent hours together on each visit. Agreed that he had personal relationships with Maitreyi and looked upon their kids as his grandchildren. But still it seemed far-fetched for a chief minister or his family to entertain an old guard so much. Ajay also realised that the Chief Minister was no more his congenial self, but he had to try and ask all the questions he had brought with himself. So, he continued to ask him if he know anything about his life before Rajan Chaudhari came to the city.

Chief Minister denied any knowledge about it, saying that Rajan was always very secretive about his personal life. He did not want any interference or inquisitiveness and hence he had never asked him.

Ajay found it hard to digest because in his investigation about Rajan Chaudhari over the past couple of days he had found that the one person who was closest to him was the chief minister himself. He was rumoured to have spent days on end in his house before his marriage to Maitreyi. It was not practically possible to not have interacted with his family members, be it his wife or the kids, at all. But Ajay knew where to draw the line. He stopped the questions and took his leave.

On his way back to the police station, Ajay kept thinking about his interview with the chief minister. Something did not sound right. Everyone he had talked with since the murder had said that he was the closest person to the victim and the best one to provide any information. But he had refused to discuss anything personal about him. He in fact alleged he did not know anything about his native place as well and now Ajay was stumped.

Nearly a week into the investigation, the forensic reports began to land on Ajay's desk. As Ajay pored over the reports, the nuances started to make themselves clear. Dr. Mehta, the senior forensic scientist, had detailed the gunshot residues and angles, indicating that the shots were fired from a short distance, likely less than two meters away. The bullets were of a specific make, rarely found in street-level crimes, pointing again towards a professional hit. Even the way the motorcycle's tire marks were left suggested a machine well-maintained; no amateur would have such attention to detail. All these elements echoed the hallmarks of a carefully planned assassination, one that left no room for failure.

In the Panvel case, a wealthy businessman named Rohit Desai had been the victim. Rohit was known to be punctual and followed a rigid daily schedule. His assailants had exploited this predictability. A beggar girl had approached his car at a red light on a route he always took, and when he rolled down the window to give her some money, masked assailants struck. They grabbed his briefcase, which held sensitive documents, and before anyone could react, a motorbike that had been idling nearby sped away, weaving through the maze of traffic. The beggar girl melted away into the crowd. Investigating officer Inspector Nair noted how cleanly the operation had been executed — no violence beyond the essential, no witnesses who could give a detailed account and the beggar girl remained unfound. The only trace left was a similar tire mark that was also clean of any unique identifiers.

But it was the Ranchi murder that sent a chill down Ajay's spine. Much like Rajan Chaudhari, the victim was a local politician, an upcoming star named Sunil Yadav. A well-known social worker, he was beloved in his community, which made his murder even more shocking. Sunil had just wrapped up a rally and was headed home, his car swarmed by an adoring crowd. In that throng was a beggar woman who approached the car window, and Sunil, a man of the people, rolled down the window to give her alms. That is when a bullet pierced the air, taking Sunil's life. The investigation was led by an officer named Rekha Singh. Like Rajan, Sunil never refused alms on his way back from any public event — a small, charitable quirk that had been exploited.

Soon Rekha Singh, Inspector Nair and Ajay started a series of correspondence, sharing minute details of their respective cases, puzzling over the coincidences and chilling similarities. Were they all connected? Was it the same group or just an individual demonstrating the same modus operandi in different cities? Ajay requested both to send over the case pics. Ajay sent them to the forensics to compare with the Rajan Chaudhari case. After much painstaking comparisons, they unearthed that the bullet used in the Ranchi incident was of an identical make to the one used in Rajan Chaudhari's assassination.

And then there were the tire marks. Forensic analyst Sharma had been meticulous in documenting them, and his report highlighted the eerie similarities to the marks found in Rajan Chaudhari's case. Clean and offering only the bare minimum of information, as if deliberately sanitized to frustrate any investigation. But Sharma had found one more thing—a specific but very faint abrasion pattern on the tire mark, common to both scenes. It was not enough to identify a specific motorcycle, but it was enough to indicate that both crimes might involve the same machine or the same brand of tires.

Equipped with even more information, Ajay dove back into his investigation, the shadows of the other cases pressing into his thoughts. The forensics had spoken, and their story was unsettling. He felt like he was tracing the outlines of a ghost, a dangerous specter that knew how to strike – even if only the elite - and vanish, leaving only the barest shadow of its presence. Yet, Ajay could not shake the feeling that he was inching closer to unmasking this phantom. And in that pursuit, every detail mattered.

25-02-2018

It was getting late but still Ajay sat down at his work desk in the corner of his room before going to bed. It was his habit to look at his next day's schedule so that he was prepared for the day when he got up in the morning. Of course, most of the things were fluid and hence most of the diary was blank. However, it was the appointment that had been arranged much before that he needed to be ready for because usually, they were the ones he could not afford to miss out on. He had to go to the CM's office tomorrow evening for a briefing. It was his usual weekly in person reporting since the Assembly Bombing. Ajay realised that he would also have to brief on Rajan Chaudhari murder together with the Assembly bombing.

And then it struck him.

Chief minister was the common factor in all the three cases. He was almost a victim in the Assembly bombing. He had been present at the crime scene 2 hours before it happened in the case of Police Headquarter bombings. In the case of Rajan Chaudhari murder, he was closely related to the victim. Being a policeman Ajay was by nature doubtful of coincidences. And three coincidences were too much for him to digest. He could not bring himself to ignore it. Sleep eluded him and he pulled out his notebook and began scribbling. He listed each case and how the Chief Minister could be involved.

For the Assembly bombing and murder cases Ajay had already taken statements from him but now he would have to look at them with this new angle. He would also have to find some way of bringing up the police headquarter bombing case and ask his views on them. At that point of time nobody had thought of interviewing the Chief Minister because he had already left the premises more than 2 hours ago when the explosions occurred. Ajay also realised that he could not share his thoughts with anyone else. People will take him to be crazy or too big to fill his own shoes. Moreover, it was just a hunch and he needed solid proofs to be able to convey this to his colleagues.

It was past midnight when Ajay finally gave up scribbling on his notebook because it would not bring any results, and went to bed. But sleep would not come. He kept tossing and turning on the bed and kept looking at his watch to be able to get up without his mother asking too many questions. Finally, he dozed off to sleep and got up with a start at 6:00, his usual time. But today he was not feeling rested. Instead, it felt as if he had not slept or taken rest for the past so many days. His eyes were red due to lack of sleep and mind was heavy with myriad thoughts bombarding it every second.

The first thing that he did on getting up was open his notebook to see what was the final things he had written down. It was a list of things to do to reassess the two bombing cases. He knew that he will have to take Satyarthi's help in this because he was the expert. Without rousing his suspicions. He was a senior person and conservative in many ways. Ajay could not even imagine sharing his hunch with him. Satyarthi was sure to give him a dressing down as well as outrightly reject the idea.

Time would prove Ajay wrong on this front.

CHAPTER 8

07-03-2018

Two weeks had passed since Rajan Chaudhari's murder, and Ajay was mentally and physically drained. The case was proving to be a labyrinth with no clear exit, and the political pressure was mounting every day. When Karuna invited him to her son's birthday party, he thought it might be a good opportunity to unwind, even if just for a few hours. He loved spending time with his colleagues after duty hours. With no real family at home, they were his family.

Arriving at the celebration, he was surprised to see Satyarthi there, enjoying the festivities with his family. He soon found out that Kusum, Satyarthi's sister, was her college friend. Ajay's heart skipped a beat. Because that meant Kusum would be there too. Kusum was a chapter from his own past, a chapter filled with laughter, deep brown eyes, and love-lit faces—a chapter he thought he had closed but had just been reopened.

Since Ajay had started working with Satyarthi on the Assembly bombing case, he had had a few chance encounters with Kusum, but they were just that. Fleeting appearances in each other's line of sight. But now it seemed they would be in proximity for a good amount of time.

"Hey Ajay, it's been a while! Let us catch up," Satyarthi said, pulling him to a quieter corner of the garden where they could talk.

"Definitely. How have you been?" Ajay managed, all the while stealing glances at Kusum, who was busy with other guests.

"Busy, just like you. I have been following your recent case—the Rajan Chaudhari murder. That is some serious stuff, isn't it?" Satyarthi sipped his drink and looked intently at Ajay, as if trying to read him.

Ajay felt a tug of professional duty pull him back to the present moment. "Yes, it's a complicated case. I have been trying to connect the dots, but there are just too many variables. And there are similarities to other past cases, which might indicate a larger conspiracy."

Satyarthi raised an eyebrow, clearly intrigued. "That sounds like an unfolding political thriller. Any suspects in mind yet?"

Ajay hesitated. He wanted to share his growing suspicion about the Chief Minister, who was a common thread in all three cases. Just as he was about to voice his thoughts, laughter echoed from across the garden. Kusum. Ajay's train of thought derailed instantly. The way she laughed, her eyes sparkling, her face glowing with happiness—it all rushed back to him in flashes, momentarily sweeping him away from the case, Satyarthi and the party around him.

Satyarthi noticed Ajay's wandering attention and followed his gaze to where Kusum was standing. His eyes narrowed slightly, a complex mix of emotions momentarily flashing across his eyes. "Ah, Kusum. Ever the life of the party, isn't she?"

Ajay felt the undertone in Satyarthi's words, a subtle reminder of a chapter he had chosen to close. "Yes, she always has been," he replied softly, aware of the tension that had suddenly materialised in the air between them. Satyarthi had never completely forgiven him for breaking off his relationship with Kusum, especially when the topic of marriage had been on the table.

Caught between the resurfacing past and the pressing demands of the murder investigation, Ajay found himself at an emotional crossroads, reminded of the complexities of both love and duty.

Realizing he was losing focus, Ajay clenched his fist discreetly. "The case is ongoing, and I am not sure what details to share. Let's just say it's not as straightforward as it seems."

"Fair enough," Satyarthi nodded. "But if you ever need an outside perspective, you know where to find me."

"I'll keep that in mind," Ajay said, shaking his head. But even as he spoke, his thoughts were already drifting back to Kusum, torn between the weight of his professional obligations and the emotional undercurrents of a past that refused to stay buried. Would the night bring clarity to his muddled thoughts, or would it further deepen the maze he found himself in? Either way, Ajay knew the coming days would be pivotal — both for his heart and for the case that seemed to grow more complex by the minute.

As he watched Kusum laugh among friends, her deep brown eyes sparkling with the same effervescence that had once captivated him, Ajay's mind waded into the past. He had been a rookie in the police force back then, starry-eyed, and eager to make a difference. Marriage, to him, had appeared as a monumental commitment, a chain of responsibilities he was not ready to anchor himself to.

He had just begun to find his footing in the complex world of law enforcement, grappling with its numerous challenges, ethical dilemmas and personal sacrifices. The thought of bringing another person into this chaos, especially someone he cared for deeply, had weighed on him. He could not shake off the nagging thought that having a wife at home would make him hesitate in the line of duty, cloud his judgment with fears for her well-being. And so, he had made the difficult choice to walk away from Kusum, without fully realizing the emotional scars he would leave on both.

But tonight, when the intervening years had made him more mature, he could not help but question how different life might have been if he had made the opposite choice. Could he have balanced both worlds, one fraught with danger and the other demanding emotional availability and stability?

As Ajay stood there, letting his gaze drift from Kusum back to the room, another layer of his past unfurled in his mind — his father's abandonment and his mother's struggles to raise him alone. His mother had been a pillar of strength, working tirelessly to provide for him and his sister, but her bitterness towards his father had seeped into their home like a stubborn stain. She had often ranted about the irresponsibility and callousness of men, a generalization born from her personal heartbreak but one that had a lasting impact on young Ajay.

The words of his mother had become a kind of haunting refrain, shaping his perception of marriage and manhood. At the prospect of marriage to Kusum, he found himself wondering if he would end up repeating his father's mistakes. Could he promise to always do right by Kusum when he had witnessed firsthand how easily promises could be broken? This lack of trust in himself had added another layer of complexity to his decision to not marry Kusum. It was not just about his career or the hazards of his job; it was also about the emotional baggage he carried, baggage filled with his mother's disillusionment and his father's absence.

Now, watching Kusum radiant with laughter and life, he could not help but wonder what had been lost because of his decision. The room was full of merriment, the air tinged with the smell of delicious food and the sound of joyful conversations, but for Ajay, it all blurred into the background. As his investigative mind sought to unravel the complexities of Rajan Chaudhary's murder, his emotional self was grappling with the complexities of love and commitment. And in that moment, each seemed as puzzling and elusive as the other.

He refocused his attention, anchoring himself back to the urgency of the case. But as he did, he realized that the questions that swirled around his personal life were not ones that could be neatly filed away like the evidence or clues in an investigation. They were messy, intricate and unending — much like the way he still felt about Kusum.

With a sigh and strong willpower, Ajay brought himself back to the reality. A reality where he and Kusum were strangers and he had a duty to fulfil towards his host. He went back inside the house where the party was in full swing, and tried to be his usual affable self. When he started for home, Karuna pressed a box of sweets in his hands: "For your children Sir. They are dry. Give them when you meet them next." Ajay smiled to himself; she must have found out.

CHAPTER 9

08-03-2018

Even after poring over the reports and scrutinizing the facts from every possible angle, Ajay found himself at an impasse. There was not much to go on and he kept circling back to the same thought – that the chief minister was the common thread in both the cases. His gut told him that he should not let go of that one thing he had, however flimsy or outlandish. After all, he could not really implicate the chief minister in a crime. Or could he?

Finally, after much deliberation, or probably because he could think of nothing better, Ajay assigned constable Tukaram to investigate any incidents that had recently occurred around the Chief Minister – a shooting, an explosion, sudden interruption on road, anything that seemed design to harm him or those around him.

"Given the recent bombing near the assembly and the murder of his mentor, we need to ensure that the CM isn't the next target," he told the constable, who looked convinced by the logic. It was an election year, after all; everyone was on high alert.

The assignment had a side benefit Tukaram had not anticipated: he was excused from field duty to focus on research. As much as he relished the adrenaline of chasing down leads in the field, he could not deny the sense of relief that came with being spared from the never-ending emergency calls that often turned out to be false alarms. Civilians spooked too easily these days, and their hypervigilance often led to dead ends that sucked up precious time and resources.

However, digging into incidents surrounding the Chief Minister was like looking for a needle in a haystack. Newspapers and websites were saturated with mentions of him, making it a Herculean task to sieve through. On the second day, however, Tukaram flagged a titbit that excited Ajay no end: another bombing, this time at a rally the Chief Minister had attended. Miraculously (or was it intentionally, Ajay wondered) there had been no casualties, and the CM himself was unscathed. But the fact that it was another bombing raised alarms in Ajay's mind.

Ajay listened intently as the constable relayed further details about the incident. "Compile a full report on that rally incident," he said. "Include photocopies of all relevant newspaper articles you can find. Lay them out chronologically, and do not miss a detail. I want that on my desk by tomorrow evening."

Tukaram looked at him with his eyes widening ever so slightly. He was clearly sensing the urgency Ajay felt but could not fully comprehend. Ajay could not share his hunch with Tukaram, so dismissed him. Ajay realised that the nuances of each incident mattered now more than ever when he was sure of not finding a shred of direct evidence. He needed to understand the context, the atmosphere and any subtleties that journalists might have picked up on but police reports could have ignored. He needed the public narrative as well as the official one, and he needed it all as soon as possible.

Ajay could not escape the dreaded feeling that the Chief Minister was looking more and more like the hub of a dangerous wheel. Each spoke was an incident, seemingly unrelated, but the centre was becoming increasingly difficult to ignore. He knew he was placing a lot on the line, but the stakes were higher than ever, and the mystery was begging to be unravelled. He could not let this opportunity go. Not just for the adrenalin rush that it would give him but because he firmly believed it was his duty to uphold the law despite the stature of the criminal.

11-03-2018

It was Sunday and the police station was nearly empty, operating on bare minimum staff. Ajay had decided to come to the police station that day. As he had nothing new on his desk – even criminals seemed to be taking the day off – Ajay walked into the case room and stared at the wall dedicated to the recent crimes. Pinned photographs, maps, timelines: the board was a mish-mash of recent crimes that cried out for resolution. The crime dates were written so boldly above all the boards that anyone looking towards the wall would be attracted to them. Out of the blue, Ajay was suddenly reminded of that chit of a boy at the tuition centre. The boy used to keep adding the digits of every number he came across, be it phone numbers, number plates, age, marks, whatever. Ajay also remembered suddenly that the Chief Minister was a staunch believer in numerology as well as astrology. Was not the CM himself telling him the other day frustratingly that he should have consulted the astrologer before arranging the Martyr's Day function.

On just a hunch, Ajay did the only thing he knew about numerology – it had something to do with adding all the digits of a number and making predictions or decisions based on that.

He added the dates. 30.01.2018 (30+1+11) and 20.02.2018 (20+2+11)

They came to 42 and 33.

He did not know what their relationship was, except that both were multiples of 3!

Besides Ajay, there was someone else trying to decipher a relationship. Between Ajay and Satyarthi – the two lead investigators of Assembly blast case. For lack of something new on this front, Sonia was trying to work this angle to keep her viewers hooked. She had felt something was off between the two of them on the day of the blast itself, and filed it away for later use if the need arose.

Considering her editor's constant pressure, she felt the time had come. If Ajay and Satyarthi couldn't solve the case in these six weeks, they should be ready to become subjects of investigation themselves! A quick background check revealed that Ajay's seconding posting was at Urangarh, in the same police station as Satyarthi. That too for three long years. After that this was the first time they had received posting in the same city.

In the short time that Sonia had worked the crime beat, she had developed her own contacts. She called one of them and explained what she wanted. Two days later she went to meet the old constable her contact had recommended. Laden with 2kgs of sweets, because that was all he wanted in exchange for information. After spending an hour with the constable, Sonia felt it was money well spent. She had gathered enough dirt to keep things moving for a couple of weeks.

The next day her on-air segment was plastered with images of Satyarthi, Ajay and the Urangarh police station where they worked together. In true blue journalist style, she alluded to a rift between the two dating back to their Urangarh posting without giving too much detail. She could have easily mentioned Kusum, but something held her back. She did not want to reveal all her cards at the same time. She wanted to keep it newsy longer. Sonia just flashed a few images of the police lines, where both had lived, and left it at that. To the viewers' imagination.

Over the next couple of days, she kept releasing juicy titbits about Ajay and Satyarthi. And to everyone's relief Kusum's name or a hint of the two hooking up had not yet featured there. Other news channels had also picked up on the news but it was obvious they were simply regurgitating Sonia's version, without any research of their own.

28-03-2018

Almost two weeks had passed since Sonia's first news item on Ajay and Satyarthi. Ajay felt embarrassed each time he came across Satyarthi. To Satyarthi's credit, he maintained a stoic demeanour with him. But Ajay's heart constricted each time he remembered what Kusum must be going through. Living on tenterhooks as to when the big reveal might come from Sonia. Assuming she knew about it. But the thing is, when we are in a fix, we tend to assume the worst. Many times, he picked up the phone to call her up (he was glad Kusum had not changed her number since then), but then lost the courage to go through with it. What will he say to her?

Plus, the case was keeping him fully occupied. And he didn't have much time for personal things, at least when he was at work.

After one such tiring and mentally exhausting day, when Ajay reached home, the front door was unlocked. His jaw tightened and a shadow passed over his face but he collected himself quickly and pressed the doorbell. He could hear the footsteps shuffling slowly inside the house and almost shouted for her mother to come quickly. As he bent down to touch her feet, her mother grunted and nodded her head. That was all.

While Ajay showered, he tried to imaging why his mother might have come. It had been more than three years since she had visited him, and first for this posting. He wondered what had pushed her to leave the comfort of her home and travel all the way here. At least she had come when she had. If she had come even a week earlier, she would have deciphered what Sonia had failed to spell out till now. Just then she called out from kitchen, "come out fast if you want hot chapatis," and that put to rest his speculation. At least he would have some hot and tasty home-cooked food while she was here.

Ajay's mother had made his favourite *kheer*, a sweet dish made of rice cooked in milk and garnished with dry fruits, and *pancharatan daal,* lentil made of five varieties of pulses. He relished the food while his mother continued a monologue. He showed ample interest by making the right noises at the right places just so she would let him eat in peace. When his tummy felt almost full, he made the mistake of asking, "how is Roshni?" and his mother launched into an animated monologue on how she had become very selfish of late and had no time even for her own mother. He wanted to remind her that Roshni's in-laws' health had deteriorated and she needed to spend more time caring for them. Also, her elder daughter was in Class 9 and needed more supervision in her studies. But Ajay refrained from saying anything. As she stayed near her daughter's place, she would know of all this more than Ajay, but she never cared. That was the way his mother had become ever since his father had disappeared – always thinking of herself and how she had done so much for everyone but now no one had time for her. Even after so many years he longed for the kind, loving and warm-hearted lady she used to be. With a sigh he got up and excused himself saying he had some paperwork to complete.

He spent the next 2-3 hours reading the three case files – Assembly bombing, Rajan Chaudhari murder and Police HQ bombing. He made copious notes and scribbled out his ideas pages after pages in his notebook. He was looking for patters. For patterns it always was, if the cases were related. And he had the gut feeling that they were related. He just needed to find the pattern. That first thread that linked the three of them. And may be a fourth one, the bomb explosion in the rally last year, which Tukaram had unearthed. He will have more to go on when he had the file on that. And may be something else too if Tukaram found some more clues. Yes, he was searching for clues without having an inkling of how critical his research was.

CHAPTER 10

08-04-2018

It was again a Sunday but today Ajay was not going to the Police Station. He had to go to the tuition centre where he taught children for free. Their exams were coming and he had promised to be with them the whole day. Nandini, the tuition centre owner, had called her up yesterday to confirm and he had given his assent. He had also thought that if he didn't go to the Police Station he would be able to return home earlier and take his mother to a few places for sightseeing.

But Ajay did not tell his mother about any of his plans for the day. He did not want to spoil his Sunday. He knew that as soon as he said anything, she would invariably launch into another scathing monologue about how he cared only about others and not his own mother. She would happily forget that they would be spending the afternoon together and remember only that he gave a couple of hours to those unfortunate children. So he decided it was best to keep quiet and make it look like a last minute thought.

Teaching underprivileged children had been Ajay's pet project since his first posting. He taught for free those children who could not afford expensive tuitions. He himself had been a good student and loved sharing his knowledge with others, which showed in the sparkle of his eyes and passion in his voice when he stood at the blackboard. He tried to keep in touch with those children who needed guidance and support, because they had no one to do so. Typically, these turned out to be fatherless kids who were good in studies. From every posting he had kept in touch with one or two such kids. Ajay seemed to be gathering his own kind of tribe.

It was while teaching the students that day that Ajay got his breakthrough. As it was exam time, some of the younger kids had also turned up. He was teaching them the divisibility rules and for 9 he said this – keep adding the digits till you get a single digit. If you get 9, the given number is divisible by 9, else it is not. Keep adding till you get a single digit. A lightning struck him.

He whipped out his smartphone and started typing furiously – how do you use numerology. And within seconds he had millions of pages telling him how to use numerology for everything from career and marriage to buying homes and planning kids. The one thing that stood out on the scores of pages he skimmed was this – you must keep adding the digits till you obtain a single digit. So, the numbers were not 33 and 15. They were 6. Same number. May be a lucky number for the Chief Minister. Now if the rally explosion date also added up to 6, it would be a definite pointer to the Chief Minister.

Ajay had to exercise supreme control over himself not to bolt out of the classroom and go look for that date. He finished the classes, cleared every one of their doubts and only then went home. He was glad he had not shared his plans with his mother. He would have hated to cancel.

Once he reached home, Ajay went straight to his writing desk and like a maniac rummaged through his drawer to find the file that Tukaram had given him. He had kept all papers related to his "hunch" on the CM at home. With trembling hands, he wrote down the date on the piece of paper. When it added up 6, he did not know whether he should give a whoop of joy or pull at his hair in despair. It would not be easy to explain this stuff – numerology to be precise – to Wankhede, or even Satyarthi.

As far as Ajay was concerned, this connected the chief minister with all these crimes and explosions but he was not sure that anybody would be willing to listen to him. Yes, they all had seen weirdest of crimes being committed all their lives, but this was not an ordinary crime or criminal he was talking about. He was talking about the highly respected, learned and loved Chief Minister of the state. He was also talking of bombings in high profile places like the Police HQ and the Assembly. Even after racking his brains for hours, he was nowhere near answering the most pertinent questions. What next? He had found the pattern but now he needed to find the evidence because evidence was something everybody could see; hunch and hypothesis was nothing without evidence. And forget about the court, first he needed to convince his colleagues and the police commissioner.

Under the guise of security, Ajay put on surveillance at the CM's residence. Nothing elaborate. The team reported to him after a couple of days that the Chief Minister was due to make a trip outside the city. They wanted to know if they needed to continue the surveillance even there. Lots of logistics would need to be worked out and hence they wanted to know beforehand. Now Ajay was in a fix, because he was doing all this without any formal plan or permission from the department. Providing security within the city could be a good excuse but there was no excuse to send extra people when the Chief Minister was travelling outside because then he would not be responsible for providing security. Ajay asked his men to find out where he was going from the house staff. They could reveal something unwittingly.

This trick worked and Ajay got to know that the Chief Minister was in the habit of visiting the Kamakhya Temple every month. On these visits he did not take his family or even his secretary with him. This piqued Ajay's interest even further because it seemed like something new or different from a routine expected of any chief minister. Chief ministers' repertoire is always packed and to find time every month to visit a temple thousands of kilometres away seemed strange. There must be something extremely important there that could not be left to others. But every month? Ajay knew he just had to find this out. Since it was not possible to do this under the garb of CM's security, he had to find a different way of tackling this problem. And he did.

Ajay's mother had been feeling restless of late. She probably wanted to go home but was in double mind. She had got, or rather realised she will not get, what she had come for. It was Ajay's guess that she had come to talk of his marriage but having seen Kusum at the function that day she knew it was futile to broach the topic. The local rotary club had organised their annual glitterati event for the police department and he had taken his mother with him. It was a mistake, Ajay realised later, because Kusum was also present there.

In a way Ajay was relieved. Seeing Kusum in the office all those weeks ago had rekindled feelings he had long assumed dead. And this was not at all the right time for his mother to approach the topic of his marriage. He needed to explore his own feelings, understand what he wanted and what was possible before coming to any decision.

Ajay took a week's leave and then broached the topic with his mother. He said that he had got 2 days' leave and if she wanted he could accompany her back home. He would be able to meet Roshni as well; it had been quite a long time since they had met. Though what Ajay said was right, his mother looked at him with suspicion. It was quite unlike Ajay to offer to drop her home. She knew there must be something else underway but still decided to go with Ajay's plan. Which was actually to drop her home, meet Roshni and proceed to Kamakhya temple from there.

10-05-2018

The air was hot and heavy in Kamakhya. Ajay, blending seamlessly with the pilgrims, found himself a discreet spot in the temple's periphery, giving him a vantage point to monitor the chief minister's movements. Though it was a temple, and a revered one at that, for Ajay, it was just another stakeout. He had learned over the years that the most seemingly innocent of places could harbour the deepest of secrets.

The sun cast long shadows across the temple complex as it began its descent. Ajay watched the chief minister throughout the day. The man seemed genuine in his devotion, with no signs of pretence. He participated in all the temple rituals with a fervour that surprised Ajay. The entire day, the CM seemed like any other devout pilgrim, seeking blessings and engaging with the temple priests.

As evening turned to night, the temple grounds slowly emptied. The hymns and chants faded, replaced by the sound of crickets and the distant howl of the wind. And yet, the chief minister showed no signs of leaving.

Determined not to lose sight of him, Ajay carefully maneuvered closer. The temple lights cast eerie shadows, and the atmosphere was heavy with the scent of incense and the evening's offerings. Time seemed to stretch endlessly. Ajay fought the weight of his eyelids, keeping himself awake with sips of water and the constant reminder of the importance of his mission.

Close to midnight, as the moon hung high and silvery, illuminating the temple's ancient stones, Ajay's patience paid off. The chief minister, who had been seated in a secluded corner with a rosary in hand, got up and walked slowly towards the temple's inner sanctum. His security detail remained at a distance, respecting the sanctity of the place.

Ajay's heart raced. He had expected the CM to maybe engage in some private prayer or a secret ritual, but what unfolded was completely unexpected. The temple's head priest, a formidable figure in saffron robes, met the chief minister at the entrance of the sanctum sanctorum. They exchanged a few words, and then, both went inside, disappearing from Ajay's view.

The minutes that followed felt like hours. The silence was palpable, broken only by the occasional chirping of a night bird or the rustling of leaves. Ajay's mind raced with possibilities. What were they discussing? Was it something related to the crimes? Or perhaps a personal confession?

After what felt like an eternity, the door to the sanctum opened. The chief minister stepped out first, his face unreadable in the moonlight. He looked neither content nor troubled. The head priest followed shortly after, his gaze distant, lost in some profound thought.

Ajay remained still, processing what he had witnessed. The chief minister's midnight rendezvous with the temple's head priest was indeed unusual, especially given the security risks involved. This had to mean something, and Ajay was determined to uncover the truth behind this enigmatic meeting.

The next steps were clear in his mind. He had to find out more about the head priest and the nature of his relationship with the chief minister. The mystery had deepened, and Ajay was now more committed than ever to unravel it. But first he needed to examine the temple more closely.

A new day brought with it a fresh wave of pilgrims to the Kamakhya Temple, which was a boon for Ajay. As the morning rituals commenced, he merged with the crowd in his casual attire. He had swapped his usual formal look for that of a typical devotee tourist, complete with both garland and camera slung around his neck.

The temple, with its intricate carvings and architectural brilliance, was a photographer's delight. Tourists often snapped away, capturing memories of their visit. But Ajay's motives were different. He systematically started photographing the temple's key areas. The main entrance, the stairs and pathways leading to the inner sanctums, the locations of the guards, exit points and especially the central temple, the location of the midnight meeting. Camera was not allowed inside the *garbha griha* but Ajay managed to meticulously capture every angle, every alcove and every corridor besides that.

While most visitors aimed to capture the deity's splendour or the gleaming eyes of the temple's priest as they chanted the morning prayers, Ajay was focused on gathering more strategic images. Shots that displayed the temple's layout, the relative distance between its primary structures and possible hidden passages or doors. And yes, the head priest himself. Late in the morning, Ajay had started despairing that he wouldn't be able to capture the priest's photograph. But just then he came out with someone who looked like his junior, and stood in the courtyard chatting. Ajay managed to click several headshots and profiles of the head priest.

Taking breaks between his photography sessions, Ajay also discreetly observed the temple's daily operations. He noticed how the priests moved, the rhythm of their duties, the places they used more often and the areas they avoided. This gave him insights into the more private and restricted areas of the temple. Who knew what information might come in useful in the future.

After a few hours, once he was satisfied with the images he had collected, Ajay sat at a local tea stall, flipping through the digital photos on his camera. At first glance, they looked like any other tourist's captures. But when arranged in a specific order, they would provide a comprehensive layout of the temple complex.

Ajay knew that once he got back, he could use these photos to create a digital map, giving him a better understanding of the temple's structure. This would prove invaluable, especially if he needed to coordinate a more extensive investigation or, God forbid, a raid.

As he sipped his tea, Ajay's mind kept wandering back to the chief minister's secret meeting and the temple's enigmatic head priest. While the photos gave him a physical understanding of the temple, there still remained many unanswered questions. Why was the chief minister of a powerful state conferring with a priest in the dead of the night? What was their relationship? And more importantly, how did it tie back to the series of crimes that had rocked the city? Or, did it even tie back?

Determined and more resolute than before, Ajay made his way back to his lodgings, to prepare for the journey back and the investigation that lay ahead.

13-05-2018

Ajay wasted no time upon his return. He headed straight to his office, realising that he would not have been able to get away if someone was home. His mother or... Ajay took with him all the files related to the case, which he had been hoarding at home for safety. He needed everything together in one place now.

Ajay ordered express delivery of the print photos. He instructed Tukaram to come back only when he had the photos with him. While waiting for them he transferred all the photos from the camera to his desktop. Then he deleted the ones he had in his mobile. Once Tukaram brought the photos, Ajay spread them out on his desk, each snapshot forming a piece of the puzzle. With a magnifying glass he scrutinized the head priest's image, searching for any discerning feature, any scar or mark that could identify him. While the beard effectively concealed most of the priest's face, the intensity of his eyes was unmistakable. There was a story there, and Ajay was determined to uncover it.

Opening up the image on his computer, Ajay used the software to scan and match it against a comprehensive police database containing records of criminals, missing persons, and other individuals of interest from the past two decades.

The first search yielded no results. Ajay was not surprised, considering the beard's concealing nature. With a few deft clicks, he used the software to digitally erase the beard, revealing the priest's face beneath. Running the search again, the computer whirred and beeped before displaying a match.

The moment a face started appearing on the screen, Ajay whistled, a reflex whenever he made a crucial breakthrough. But when it appeared fully, he felt a mix of emotions – the thrill of discovery, coupled with a sinking feeling of despair. He did not recognize the man though he knew the name. The man was one of the most wanted figures of India. He had disappeared decades ago without a trace, leaving the police of many states baffled. Many believed he had died or fled the country, but here he was, masquerading as a holy figure in a revered temple. Why? What were his designs? And how was the chief minister connected with him?

The discovery raised more questions in Ajay's mind than answered them. Ajay realized the stakes had just risen many notches. This case was no longer just about patterns or numerology; it was about digging deep into the past and confronting the ghosts that lay there. Ajay leaned back, closing his eyes briefly, gathering his thoughts. The game was on, and it was about to get even more intense. But he needed an ally.

CHAPTER 11

14-05-2018

Eyes heavy with lack of sleep, Ajay paced around his dimly lit office, feeling the weight of the information he had gathered. Each clue, each piece of evidence, interlinked intricately to tell a story so implausible, it seemed like a Jack Higgins potboiler. Yet, he could not ignore the nagging voice inside his head that whispered that it was all true. He recognized the need for collaboration, an ally who could help him sift through the bizarre narrative he had constructed. Approaching the police commissioner was out of the question; presenting such an unbacked tale would risk ridicule or, worse, professional suicide. It was Satyarthi, Ajay concluded, who he needed by his side. An experienced officer, Satyarthi would be the voice of reason to his speculations, grounding him as they navigated this perplexing case. Had he not been decent with him till now? Despite the mess he had created all those years ago? Even after he had caught him checking out Kusum at Karuna's party? Even after Sonia's news item? Satyarthi had been his mentor and idol once, how could he doubt his intentions.

So, taking a deep breath, Ajay picked up his phone and dialled Satyarthi's number. The call was brief, with Ajay simply asking if Satyarthi could drop by his office later that evening. He emphasized the need for utmost discretion and requested that they be left undisturbed for the duration of the conversation. They settled on a time post office hours, when the department would be mostly empty.

As Satyarthi walked in to Ajay's office that evening, his face was a mask of curiosity and slight concern. Without much preamble, Ajay began laying out his case. Starting from his initial suspicion surrounding the Chief Minister, to the startling revelations about the dates of the various crimes, he left out no detail. He described his undercover trip to the Kamakhya Temple, producing the pictures of the priest, leading up to the bombshell revelation that the very priest might be one of the five radicals from the village of Saado.

Satyarthi's reactions evolved as the story unfolded. What started as a slight smirk of scepticism slowly transformed into wide-eyed disbelief. By the end, Satyarthi seemed visibly shaken, leaning back in his chair, absorbing the gravity of the situation. He agreed that this needed more investigation, emphasising the importance of hard evidence before accusing someone as influential as the Chief Minister. They also acknowledged the inherent danger of the situation; if their suspicions were true and the news leaked prematurely, they could be placing their whole career, and probably life, in jeopardy.

Especially since Sonia had started taking up this case as a symbol of the police's incompetence. While Ajay was on leave, she had barged in Satyarthi's office asking for the latest official update on Assembly bombing as he was the "official" spokesperson for the case. Satyarthi had no idea who had given her this information. She had also tried to draw him on his and Ajay's relationship, both personal and professional, but Satyarthi was an old warhorse. He had managed to hold her at bay. But for how long, he had wondered.

A momentary silence settled between them, as the weight of what had been shared settled in. After a few moments, Satyarthi finally spoke up, "Ajay, if even half of what you're saying turns out to be true, we're onto something massive. But the implications are frightening."

Ajay nodded, "I know. That is why I wanted to rope you in before taking any further steps. Two heads are better than one, especially in a matter this sensitive. And officially we are still working together on the Assembly Bombing case"

Satyarthi ran a hand through his hair, "The village of Saado... Hmm...I had heard about it during my training days. An old revolutionary hub. But connecting that to our current Chief Minister? It's surreal."

For lack of any other lead to follow, Ajay and Satyarthi decide to go to Saado. It was believed to be a ghost from the past, a mere relic of a bygone era. The stories talked about the extremist movement in the 1960s, driven by a group of five youths. These young men had visions of an egalitarian society, devoid of the rampant exploitation by the zamindars. As years passed, the movement either died out or went underground, depending on who you asked. But Ajay's revelations hinted at the latter.

Both Ajay and Satyarthi decided to visit Saado to see if it held any clue. They did not hope for much, but there seemed to be no other alternative. Reaching the village was not so straightforward. They had to first take a train to Ranchi, then a bus to the nearest town, and then rely on whatever mode of transport was available to reach Saado. Since they were travelling undercover, they could not really take the help of local police or government machinery to make it easier for them.

22-05-2018

Ajay and Satyarthi were surprised that reaching the village was not as difficult as they had assumed. Though the roads were not in a very good condition, they were quite serviceable and buses were easily available till Saado. But the village itself held more surprises for them. They had got down two stops earlier and then walked all the way to Saado. They did not want to attract attention. By all accounts Saado was a tiny hamlet located on a hill surrounded by thick forests. They had expected a rudimentary, primitive village caught in a time warp. Instead, they found a village that was modern yet held an old-world charm. The cemented houses, Dish TV antennas and the biogas units defied their expectations. The village infrastructure indicated that it had moved with the times, albeit in its own unique way. The unlocked doors and communal aura gave them the sense that the village was more of an extended family. There were not that many young men and women visible; only old women lining the road and children playing on the roads without any care in the world. The young men and women were probably out working, in the fields, forests or towns nearby.

Their exploration eventually led them to a slightly isolated house, bigger and better kept than the others. There was something about the house – windowless shiny walls, tiny locked door, a well-kept green patch that was attractive yet uninviting - that intrigued them. Their feet automatically turned in its direction, without any need for conversation. On reaching the door they were surprised to find it really was locked when no other house they had seen so far had been. The lock itself was no problem. If not a police officer, Ajay would have made an expert pickpocket.

They both stepped inside and quietly latched the door. Inside, it was less of a home and more of a war room. Maps of India, pictures of people and places, newspaper clippings, handwritten notes, etc. adorned the walls, reflecting years of collected data and planning. The centrepiece was a large photograph of the Chief Minister taking oath, the very man they suspected was tied into this intricate web of history and crime.

As Ajay looked around, taking in the enormity of their find, he felt a mix of trepidation and thrill. This was more than just a hunch now. They were on the brink of unearthing a conspiracy that could shake the very foundation of their state's political landscape. But with such high stakes came immense danger, and both Ajay and Satyarthi knew they had to tread carefully.

Satyarthi turned to Ajay, his face reflecting the concern that had settled in. "You realise, Ajay, that we're venturing into a rabbit hole that could very well be deeper and darker than we can imagine."

Ajay gave a tight-lipped nod. "I've been feeling that ever since the pattern with the Chief Minister began to emerge. But now, seeing this," he gestured to the room around them, "it's clear we've just touched the tip of the iceberg."

Satyarthi moved closer to one of the walls, scanning the articles and notes, trying to connect the dots. "What surprises me is the meticulous nature of these plans. Everything seems so coordinated, so thought out. This isn't just about Saado's past; this is a well-calculated strategy for something bigger that is yet to come."

Ajay looked intently at a series of dates marked on one of the maps, "Yes, these dates here include both past and future dates. I think these are past actions that went unnoticed, or maybe were insignificant in the larger scheme of things." While talking he was also adding the numbers of the dates in his mind. Some came to 6, others did not. He concluded that the Chief Minister was not the only one calling the shots here.

Satyarthi paused, his fingers tracing the outline of the Chief Minister's photo. "Why him? Why is the Chief Minister, a man revered by one and all, at the centre of all this? Who the hell is he? Is he really what we know him to be?"

Ajay took a deep breath, "That's what we need to find out. And we need to act fast. If our hunches are correct, and the Chief Minister or the group behind him is planning something on one of these marked dates, we don't have the luxury of time."

The urgency weighed heavily on them. But amidst the gravity of the situation, there was also a determination. Both men knew that they were potentially standing against a colossal adversary, and the journey ahead would test their limits. But they were resolute in their quest for the truth.

They both whipped out their phones and began clicking pics like mad. They could not remove anything that would give them away. Tell others that someone was here. They knew that if anyone discovered an intrusion, it could be disastrous.

The duo worked swiftly, because they knew they did not have much time. Anyone could come in any moment, and there was no place to hide there. As they stepped out of the house, the village's quiet ambiance felt even more haunting, making them wonder how many secrets were buried underneath the peaceful facade.

"We need to dive deeper, Ajay," Satyarthi said, his voice low but firm with resolve. "It's not just about connecting the dots anymore. It's about unravelling a web that's been years in the making."

Ajay felt relieved on hearing these words. He had feared that Satyarthi might want to give it up to the higher authorities and back down. But now he felt bolstered by his words and added, "And we must ensure that justice prevails, no matter who stands in its way."

CHAPTER 12

25-05-2018

Ajay and Satyarthi came back with tons of photographs, using which they could reconstruct what they had observed and what their first impression was. They had also read the notes and paper cuttings stuck on the walls of that house while taking their pics. Ajay had wanted to bring back some of them as proof but Satyarthi stopped him from doing so. Taking away something would have attracted attention immediately. Photographs were enough of a proof to start with. They did not want to alert anyone to their line of investigation. The condition of the house made it obvious that there was someone taking care of it and ensuring that it was well kept.

Ajay agreed but still he wished he could have brought away something. The photograph of the paper cuttings and notes that they had brought was enough to incriminate or at least book the people involved. But that would not suffice for Ajay and Satyarthi. For one, they would need to establish the ownership of the house to identify the culprit. Experience told them that it might be registered in the name of someone innocent or someone who had already died. Also, arresting the owners would not establish any connection between the chief minister and the movement that was supposed to be long dead.

They needed to use the current crimes – murder as well as bomb explosions – to find some proof against the chief minister. At least enough to convince the police commissioner that they needed a showdown with the chief minister and listen to what he had to say to the allegations.

This meant that they had to go back to where they had started – investigate the crimes but with a new approach and an eye for some hidden clue or detail. The first thing that Ajay and Satyarthi did was order an in-depth background check of all the people involved in these three cases. It helped that Satyarthi was the investigating officer of the police HQ bombing. The fourth one that had been dug up by Tukaram was an old case, and had happened outdoors, so Ajay did not think it would add anything new or valuable. But still, since it was a bomb explosion, Satyarthi volunteered to take it up.

Ajay put Karuna in charge of the investigation, with Tukaram as the close aide. He was glad that he was no longer reporting daily to the CM, and that too in person. It would have been difficult to remain calm and composed in front of him. He expected the background check to bring in some results. People are always the most valuable assets for any network or secret group but also the weakest link. More so in case of movements where loyalty, and by inference secrecy, to the cause is deemed the most important.

At the end of just three days Karuna handed him a heavy file of 200+ people. Thankfully she had also prepared a separate file listing salient information such as age, place of birth, educational qualifications, university details, job details in a separate file. It must have taken a lot of manoeuvring and arm twisting and convincing on her part to get so much information so quickly. Although some people in the police department were already adept at using computers and preferred to use them because of speed and accuracy, some were still caught in time warp and preferred hard copies; printouts and photocopies were their mantra still. So whether Karuna received a hard copy or a soft copy of information depended upon the person who was sending them.

Ajay and Satyarthi decided to go through the summarised file before diving into the detailer dossier. Ajay worked on his laptop whereas Satyarthi used Ajay's desktop. Together they extracted a list of around 50 people who seemed likely to have crossed the chief minister's path and dived deeper into their detailed file. This they did together using the projector attached to the desktop, to save on time. Both of them combing the file separately would have needed more hours.

The fifth day brought the breakthrough they were waiting for. Ajay could not help whistling when he saw what he had. The librarian of the Assembly turned out to be from Saado. Although none of her prominent details mentioned the name of the place, there was a caste certificate she had taken from the *Mukhiya*, the village headman, and he had mentioned the name of the village. This supported Ajay's theory that the network of people must be a close-knit group related to the village of Saado. Ajay updated Satyarthi that it was the librarian who was with Chief Minister when the electricity outage had happened on 29th January. In fact, she had been the one to inform the vendor to get the electricity restored. Also, she had been on leave on 30th Jan, the day of Assembly blast.

Both Ajay and Satyarthi were buoyed up by this discovery, because finally they had something concrete to go on. They started looking into the Chief Minister's daily movement over the past year, going backward from the Assembly bombing. This was a potentially risky route to take because someone might inform the CM of it. Even if they were doing it on the pretext of Chief Minister's enhanced security arrangements, anyone who had penetrated the police department on the behest of the Chief Minister would find this unusual and report. Ajay was of the theory that this secret organisation had people in all the important and high places, so police department had to have someone from their side.

However, Ajay still decided to take the chance. He was also hoping that the Chief Minister or his group's leaders would get flustered that someone was on his tracks and end up doing something stupid, hence exposing the CM or themselves. Ajay could already establish that the chief minister and the librarian together had ensured that whoever was planting the bombs in the Assembly got sufficient time to do so.

But what was still missing was the motive. Why did the Chief Minister want a bomb explosion in the Assembly? Or for that matter the police headquarters? Or why would he get his own mentor murdered? What could be bigger than becoming the CM or potentially the PM of the country? Why would he jeopardise his such a well-protected position by undertaking petty things? Ajay realised that these were some of the questions only the chief minister could answer, but he could not barge into his room and start questioning him on those lines.

The chief minister's movement record was a veritable minefield of information if you knew what to look for. There were many gaps when no one knew where he was. Or what he was doing. Strange scenario for any Chief

Minister from security perspective. Looking at the pattern they could also pinpoint the times when he must have gone on his monthly visit to the priest at the Kamakhya Temple.

As the dossier kept getting thicker and thicker, it began looking inevitable that they would have to tell the police commissioner what they had unearthed. Fixing up a meeting with Mr Wankhede was not difficult. Convincing him of the chief minister's culpability would be. Again, the responsibility of telling the story fell to Ajay. Satyarthi joked that Ajay had experience of reciting the story!!

05-06-2018

Like Satyarthi, the commissioner was sceptical to begin with. But as the story progressed and they reached the point of visiting Saado, the look of disbelief left him. It seemed as if he was expecting someone to bring this up sooner or later. It distracted Ajay but he did not stop telling the details. Later Satyarthi would confess that he was also surprised that the Commissioner seemed to be prepared for what was coming.

Once Ajay had finished, there was a deep silence in the room. The Commissioner had the photographs in his hands but he seemed to be deep in thought and neither of them had the courage to interrupt him.

After what seemed like a long time but was just 5 minutes, Mr Wankhede asked them what they wanted. Both Ajay and Satyarthi were taken aback. The look of disbelief on their faces must have given away their thoughts, because Mr. Wankhede gave the faintest of smiles. Both had expected to be cross questioned and probed on their theory. Instead, here was the police commissioner asking if they had a plan in place to get hold of the chief minister. They remained silent for some time as if considering what to speak.

The questioning looks in the eyes of Ajay and Satyarthi was something that could not be ignored for long. Mr. Wankhede told them that he was not surprised because he knew Mr. Kaale, the erstwhile police commissioner, who had been killed in the police headquarter bombing, was on the trail of someone very powerful in politics. On that fateful day he had received a call from an informer and rushed out in a huff without telling anyone where he was going. This revelation not just shocked both Ajay and Satyarthi but also added yet another piece to the list of puzzles to be solved. But again, what was missing was the motive. Even the Commissioner could not help them in this.

Finally, the three of them decided that it would be best to fix up a meeting immediately. The commissioner was also worried that an investigation of Chief Minister's itinerary could have potentially alerted him. Ajay called up Naveen and got an appointment for the next day at 3:30 pm. After putting down the phone Ajay wondered if Naveen was a part of all this, or innocent. It was difficult to imagine the CM planning or doing anything without him.

06-06-2018, 3:25 PM

The next day was a typical hot and sticky June Day, reminding everyone that the Monsoons were knocking on the doors. Ajay and Satyarthi spent the morning locked up in Ajay's office, discussing how they will start talking to the chief minister. When the time came for them to go, they were not sure if they were ready. But the moment they put on their peak caps, they were confident of doing the right thing by the people of the country, who reposed so much faith in them.

Their names were entered for meeting at the gates of CM's residence. The security guard called up someone inside and then nodded at them to proceed. Ajay was used to all the elaborate mechanisms but today he felt it was taking unnecessarily delaying the meeting.

Naveen was waiting for them near the lawns. This was a first for Ajay. In all his visits he never had Naveen come to receive him. He was meeting Satyarthi for the first time and Ajay made the necessary introductions. They then proceeded through the lawns to the CM's residential office. Ajay was looking at everything with new eyes, while Satyarthi was taking in the details like a first-time visitor.

While the three of them were some 30 feet from the office, a deafening sound was heard and the office building in front of them blew up in a huge ball of fire.

Author Bio

Shweta writes fiction, non-fiction and poetry. She has already published two non-fiction and a flash fiction collection. Shweta also writes about impact of technology on people, businesses and society. Her work has been published in Forbes Advisor, Huffington Post, NewsWeek, SheSight Magazine and more.

Besides being a writer, she is an avid reader. She loves reading thrillers as well as slice of life novels.

Other Books by Shweta

How to Live Happily Ever After

http://mybook.to/howtolivehappily

24 Hours Are Enough: A Step-by-step Guide to Time Management for Working Professionals

https://notionpress.com/read/24-hours-are-enough

Flashes From Life (A collection of flash fiction)

http://mybook.to/FlashesFromLife

www.ingramcontent.com/pod-product-compliance
Lightning Source LLC
LaVergne TN
LVHW091103150826
845673LV00002B/702

* 9 7 9 8 8 9 1 8 6 5 9 2 1 *